THANK HEAVEN!

For Pam,
Make it fun!
Renée
11/09

Thank Heaven!

A Fantasy

RENÉE
PLANK SAVACOOL

Sense of Wonder Press
JAMES A. ROCK & COMPANY, PUBLISHERS
ROCKVILLE • MARYLAND

Thank Heaven! by Renée Plank Savacool

SENSE OF WONDER PRESS
is an imprint of JAMES A. ROCK & CO., PUBLISHERS

Thank Heaven! copyright ©2007 by Renée Plank Savacool

Special contents of this edition copyright ©2007
by James A. Rock & Co., Publishers

Address comments and inquiries to:
SENSE OF WONDER PRESS
James A. Rock & Company, Publishers
9710 Traville Gateway Drive, #305
Rockville, MD 20850

E-mail:
jrock@rockpublishing.com   lrock@rockpublishing.com
Internet URL: www.rockpublishing.com

ISBN: 978-1-59663-786-3
1-59663-786-2

Library of Congress Control Number: 2007923150

Printed in the United States of America

First Edition: 2007

For Bill, Julie, Ken, Madeline,

and Mom

(with special hugs to Molly, a Border Collie mix,
who faithfully lay at my feet and wagged
her tail in unflagging encouragement)

PROLOGUE

Screams echoed throughout the Independence Mall area of Philadelphia. Pigeons soared frenetically toward safety above the midday crowd that had gathered to see the blood-covered old woman lying on the cobblestones of the street, her head held gently in an old man's arms. A teen-aged girl stood nearby, her eyes wide in horror, staring alternately at the woman in the street and at the two tough young men who roughly gripped her arm. One of them, his foul breath hot in her ear, gruffly told her, "Doan say nothin' babycakes, or you're next." She was then roughly pushed into the side of Congress Hall as the two ran swiftly away.

I had witnessed the entire event from my new perspective in Heaven and was so frightened I could barely move or breathe. That wonderful young girl trembling and crying on the famous street corner was my beloved granddaughter. My heart ached for her and for that poor injured woman lying in the street. I knew I had to do something, but what could I do? At the time, I didn't even know my way around the danged place yet. I wondered if I could gather the guardian angels or charge on down there by myself. What the blazes were the rules in this place? What could I possibly do? It would have to be *something*. No way would I just loll around Heaven while that sweet girl was in trouble. No way!

But there I go as usual, leaping before looking, tossing the proverbial cart way ahead of the equally proverbial horse. It's time to back up and punt, take a deep breath, get it out in correct order. I must attempt to do as I am often advised: I must start at the beginning.

CHAPTER 1

The area between Fifth and Sixth Streets on Chestnut Street in Philadelphia, Pennsylvania, is one of the most famous in the United States. The area hosts tens of thousands of visitors from around the world each year. Here, under the ancient trees surrounding solid brick buildings bordered by cobble-stoned narrow side streets, is Independence Mall, where one can walk through such buildings as Independence Hall, Carpenter's Hall, and nearby Old Christ Church. In Liberty Bell Center, one can view the famous Liberty Bell and learn of its incredible history. It is in this most historic area that one can enjoy a ride in a horse-drawn carriage as part of a mini-tour of the area guided by students from the local universities or by retirees. Lucky visitors might see Benjamin Franklin—statesman, scientist, diplomat, writer, inventor, and publisher—as he strolls around the area, his little glasses perched jauntily at the tip of his nose, his brown wispy shoulder-length hair blowing in a gentle breeze off of the Delaware River. And it is to this historical site that thousands of school children flock in their hired buses each and every year, sent with teachers' hopes of instilling a sense of history into young minds and hearts.

***

The woman appeared to be in her middle sixties, certainly no younger. She was small and had thinning gray hair that had obviously not been combed for a long time. She lay propped against the east side of the Public Ledger Building across Sixth Street from

Congress Hall and Independence Hall, her belongings tucked inside in a torn paper shopping bag on the sidewalk beside her. As she slept in the early morning sun, she kept one bony hand tightly wrapped around the handles of the bag, which held all she had in the entire world. It was best to hold on to it no matter that it contained simply a faded pink sweater that had hosted a major banquet for some moths and was one size too small; three empty pizza boxes, plus a collection of newspapers from as far back as two years that she used as insulation during the cold months; and her prize—the golden wedding ring that no longer fit her bent and arthritic fingers, not even her little finger. Some day she hoped to find a chain so she could wear the ring around her neck, tucked safely beneath her blouse. For now, this precious ring was firmly tied with a piece of fraying grease-encrusted string to one handle of the bag and hung on the inside where the Bad Ones wouldn't see it, where the sun would not reflect on the gold and little diamond chip, thus alerting the Bad Ones of her treasure.

Her name was Emma, her last name was no longer important to anyone except herself, if only she could remember it. And so she slept on the same corner she had occupied every morning for the past four years. It was, she thought, *her* morning corner. A fine-looking gentleman, who apparently drank a bit too much, replaced her in the afternoons, the inevitable brown paper bag tucked discreetly under the torn arm of his threadbare brown suit jacket. She liked to think of the changeover as the Changing of the Guard, the two of them as Keepers of the Corner. It was an occurrence the two repeated on a daily basis. They had never spoken during the four years they had been occupied with the corner, but they had nodded to each other and once, not so long ago, he had smiled at her. She liked that but didn't want to appear too bold and had simply nodded once again before moving on to her afternoon spot, a shaded park bench in nearby Washington Square Park.

The park was a block south on Sixth Street, past the Curtis Publishing Building, across Walnut Street. It was lovely in all seasons, Emma thought, as one would of their private home. There were a lot of wooden benches bolted to slabs of concrete with big, thick steel bolts, but lately it was especially difficult to find one on which to recline in comfort for a nice afternoon nap. Because of so many people like Emma who inhabited the city parks, it had been deemed unseemly for the tourists to see such folks sleeping in the park so very near Independence Mall. The simple solution was to install wrought-iron arm rests mid-seat on each bench. These were about four inches in height and split the eight-foot benches nicely in half, creating no small amount of discomfort for anyone foolish enough to attempt a prone position.

Emma had been quite dismayed while watching the workers install those things on *her* benches. She was, however, delighted when the workers missed two. Perhaps they had miscounted and run out of armrests. Perhaps they had merely overlooked the two benches. All she knew was, if she were quick, she could appropriate one of them for her personal enjoyment. Her favorite was the first bench on the left at the Sixth and Walnut Streets entrance to the park; the other, acceptable of course, was the second on the left just inside the Seventh and Walnut Streets park entrance. At last check, these were still the only two without armrests.

She so enjoyed walking around the park, which she did after each Changing of the Guard, looking at the lovely circular fountain in the center, watching longingly as people and pigeons ate together. Emma knew how to read and was touched each time she passed the memorial to the unknown Revolutionary War soldiers, a small but tallish wall with George Washington's statue in the front. Behind him, carved deeply into the stone, were the large words: "FREEDOM IS A LIGHT FOR WHICH MANY MEN HAVE DIED IN DARKNESS." These words were followed with those in smaller letters: "In unmarked graves within this square lie thousands of unknown soldiers of Washington's army who died of wounds and sickness during the Revolutionary War."

Without conscious thought, Emma tightened her grip on her bag once again. She was wise to clutch her belongings, such as they were. There were gangs of young people, the Bad Ones, as she thought of them, that roamed the streets of Philadelphia and who were constantly prowling for trouble and always, when sought, found it. It was as inevitable as night follows day.

***

Juan, Roger, Otis, Chun, and Mike were the major players in one of the largest gangs in their neighborhood near the Delaware River. They were known as the Hellraisers. It was an appropriate moniker. These young men had two main interests: drugs to both sell and use, and theft, most often on the run after a mugging, to support the drug business. The average age of the boys was fifteen: Juan was the eldest at seventeen and Mike, the youngest, was newly fourteen. Juan was the best at mugging; he'd been at it longer than the others, close to five years. He had learned all he knew from his two older brothers; one of his brothers was in prison for burglary (the graduate course in mugging) and the other had died from crack cocaine a week before his nineteenth birthday.

The Hellraisers had discovered that the best mug-and-run pickings were found near Independence Mall, where the rich tourists went, their eyes hanging out along with their wallets and purses. It was a ripe area, one they claimed as their own, much the same way Emma felt about her morning corner and afternoon park bench. The gang made it a point to visit the area several times a week, sending different members so no one face would inspire a cop to anything so ridiculous as an arrest or detention. Emma knew all of the faces by this time, which is why she held so tightly to her bag. She knew the gang members weren't interested in such a person as herself, but one day it might rain, or they might get bored, and she could become a target as fast as lightening. So she held on tightly.

The young men also knew Emma and made fun of her and all of those like her who, they agreed, were too stupid to know where it was at and just sat there drooling or drinking and looking dumb. It was their collective and smug opinion that some of those Street Meats didn't even have the sense to go in out of the rain.

As long as Emma and her cohorts kept their mouths shut, the Hellraisers could care less what they did. If ever one of those scumbags said anything to the wrong folks, well, there was one more serving of Street Meat that'd be dead. Simple. Easy. No sweat.

CHAPTER 2

I'd been in Heaven for eight months when I realized I was thoroughly bored and still somewhat angry. That's not a great thing to say about Heaven, but the Truth is required here. I fussed and fumed without trying to accept my current status. *The Heaven Handbook*, issued to all upon arrival, has a precise definition of Acceptance. Basically, it is the recognition and acknowledgment of the fact that you are dead and in Heaven. I had a struggle with the concept because I was annoyed at having my life interrupted just when the going was great.

As I wrestled with my conflicting emotions in preparation of Acceptance, the scene was being set on Earth for a crime that would personally affect me, cause a stir in Heaven, and challenge the talents and resourcefulness of many guardian angels. If I'd known what was in store for me, I would have had more important things on my mind than my ennui.

Getting to Heaven was interesting; I chuckle when I think about it. Of course, I hadn't found it remotely funny at the time, but in retrospect I can appreciate the macabre humor. The first several weeks after my arrival were packed full of things to do and to learn. Just learning how to maneuver around this place was an all-out time-consuming endeavor. Heaven is HUGE. The road system is a challenge. And clouds! I've never seen so many, each as soft and comfy as the next. There were family members to visit and old friends to find. I met people I'd only read about in my schoolbooks and in newspapers. (I'm here to tell you that Sir Laurence Olivier is as gorgeous here as he was when living on Earth.)

One of the first things I did after my arrival was to look for my two former husbands. I wasn't anxious to see either. Actually, I was hoping neither had come to Heaven at all. My second mate had died ten years before I did. I couldn't find him anywhere, thank goodness, even in the lower sections where the ones on probation stay for a while. It was obvious he had gone where I was convinced he'd been angling to go ever since he first drew breath. Some things are such a comfort. My first husband arrived only weeks before I did. He was definite proof that there are still some major flaws in the system. What got him here, I'll never know.

I fuddled along with my existence until this ennui, this boredom, set in. It frighteningly resembled the mid-life crisis I'd muddled through when I was forty-seven.

As I said, getting here was one of the more interesting and totally absurd things to happen to me in my entire life. It was, of course, the last thing to happen to me in my entire life. And the timing was so poor. The kids were coming to visit, my boyfriend was getting very chummy, the house was paid for, and I had just paid off the last of my root canals. Things had been looking just great and then I had to go and die.

Because the kids were coming and Ian was staying for dinner before returning to his house around the corner, I had decided to make my special veal Florentine. I had no spinach. You simply cannot Florentine anything without spinach. There is no substitute. I would have to rush to the grocery store.

"Why don't we just eat out?" Ian, my boyfriend, wanted to know. His lovely brown eyes had a permanent twinkle. At seventy-two he was totally sexy. At seventy, *I* was totally sexy.

"Because the kids will insist on bringing their kids, who will have to bring *their* kids. It's that last batch who are so unruly. To inflict all of that on an innocent group of people confined in a restaurant would be beyond rude," I said, reaching for my sweater. There was a slight chill in the late-September air. At my age, I was noticing a "slight chill" in most air. I did not like it.

"Okay, love, if you say so, but I find your family amusing," he leaned over and kissed me in a way that made me forget all about spinach and sweaters.

"Mmmm," I said, in as much as I was in any condition to do so, "maybe we could get away with putting a vitamin assortment on the table with a pitcher of nice, cold martinis and let them all just help themselves," I murmured against his neck, nibbling a little when I was finished speaking. We certainly had vitamins galore and an unusually large supply of arthritis medications.

After several moments of uninhibited groping, breathing sounds that would have alarmed my internist, and some rather sizzling kissing and hip grinding, the phone rang. (Which reminds me, I must look up Alexander Graham Bell and give him an earful.)

Ian reached behind my left ear for the phone. "Hello?" he said as he continued to rub my back. I think I was purring. "Who?" I *was* purring. "Oh, yes, just a minute." He separated his lovely body from mine and handed me the phone, one hand over the mouthpiece. "It's Rissa," he said with a smile.

"Oh, Rissa, great!" Marissa, aka Rissa, is the younger of my two granddaughters and was then a charming sixteen. I took the receiver from Ian's large, very capable sun-tanned hand and backed away to a safer, yet not as fun, distance.

"Hello, love!" I said. "Will you be coming to see me tonight with your parents?"

"Grams, I can hardly wait! That's why I called," her lovely voice said. "I just wanted to see if maybe we could maybe, possibly, hopefully, pretty please with kisses on it have veal Florentine for dinner ... if it's no trouble ... you know it's my absolute favorite!"

Well, that did it. There could be no substitute. It would have to be spinach. I had to go to the store. My libido would have to go on "hold."

Or would it? I kept my hand on the phone after returning it to the cradle, my chin down toward my ever-decreasing chest, which was alarming as it hadn't started out in any state of abundance. Ian came up behind me and put his arms around my middle. For an old cupcake, I had managed to keep a waist and I was mightily proud of it. Ian nuzzled my neck from behind. It is so very delicious when a man swoops in from behind and nuzzles your neck. It's delicious, of course, only when you know the man and know him well. Men swooping from behind can be a terrible thing otherwise. The papers were full of such awful swoopings. But Ian swooped and I swooned. What a pair we were.

"I have to go to the store," I bemoaned, my head lolling back onto his chest.

"Mmfphff," he said into my neck.

"Rissa wants the Florentine," I explained, not moving one iota, except to remove my hand from the telephone.

"Mmfphff," he repeated and continued nuzzling.

"And we could use some other things too, like fabric softener and birdseed," I said. "You just said you were low on birdseed for the wild birds in your yard." I spun around with an alacrity belying my age. What followed proved the stove is not the only place in a kitchen where boiling can occur.

A delicious interval later, I said, "I'd better get to the store now," and began to arrange my clothing into some semblance of order.

"Want me to go with you?" he asked, as he tucked his shirt back into his jeans.

And on such a question, my fate was clinched, because Ian is tall, and he would have been with me. And events would have been much different. But, alas, I said, innocently, "No, you'd better stay here in case someone else calls and plans are altered. There are far too many people in my family who don't plan past their last sneeze." I put my purse onto my shoulder. One more nuzzle, a kiss, a quick hug, and I was out the door, car keys dangling from my carousel horse key ring. "I'll be right back!" I chirped happily.

"Don't be too long!" he said, his twinkling eyes smiled at me before he shut the door.

I can hardly wait until he gets here. It was one hell of a long and rocky road I had to trip over before I met up with Ian only two years before I died. According to the Welcoming Committee schedule that goes up every Monday morning on the East Gate, Ian should be arriving in a few weeks. I can hardly wait.

I certainly had no idea on that September afternoon that I wasn't just going to the supermarket, that a much longer journey was planned for me. If I had known, what would I have done? Clung to Ian? Gone to bed? Had a cigarette, the first since I'd been hypnotized into quitting thirty-four years previously? Gotten drunk? Changed my underwear? Sat calmly in my rocking chair? Called my kids? Taken a hot-air balloon ride? There was simply nothing I could have done. **IT** would come, no matter.

The next part is embarrassing. It is not the sort of death I would have scheduled for myself. Although, given a choice, I would probably not have scheduled one at all.

As I entered the store, I picked up one of those little plastic baskets with the uncomfortable handles that always seem to sport a mandatory, wilted lettuce leaf. Plucking the offending leaf from the bottom of *my* basket, I put it into the next basket. Once the baskets were gone, I was sure the leaf would be consigned to the floor and a fresher one would begin its journey.

I hurried into the produce aisle, moving around a little monster who was "helping Mommy push a cart." Mommy paid no attention to the child as he zoomed and zigged around and over people at a speed approaching the improbable.

"Youuuuuu … whooooo! Debarelle! (me)." A voice so shrill it made shivers slither up and down my spine as it called out to me.

I turned. There she was, the woman who wanted Ian. The woman who "dropped by" his house with so many casseroles and pies that he could open a small grocery shop. He'd begun to keep all lights in the front portion of his house turned off to discourage such visits.

"Hello, Agatha. How are you?" She looked quite dreadful in her baggy sweater and dirty sneakers. Perhaps I was unknowingly tempting fate, because pretty soon I would look as dreadful as I could/would ever look.

"Fine, an' you? How's Ian?" Her three chins quivered in eager anticipation.

"I'm fine," I answered. Then, in a devilish mood (so near The End, I was really pushing it), I continued, "Everyone's coming for dinner and I didn't have any spinach for the Florentine. That's just about everyone's favorite, especially Rissa's."

"How nice." Agatha politely smiled one of those frozen-lipped numbers that manages to scrunch up the eyelids while she patiently waited until I got around to what she wanted to hear—did I know how Ian was and, if not, did that mean she should stock up on macaroni and tuna for casseroles while she was here at the store?

"Oh, and Ian is wonderful. He's waiting for me, so I'd better get going. 'Bye!"

"Mmmm, great, Rellie. Good to see you. Remember me to Ian, will you?" [In a pig's ear.]

What was going on with Agatha back there now? I'd better check it out. Casseroles can move in fast.

After Agatha launched herself dramatically down the produce aisle, I headed directly to frozen foods. The fresh spinach was already gone, frozen would have to do.

"Howie! Where *is* that boy? How ... eeeeee!" The piercing tones of what I assumed to be his mother echoed throughout the store, bouncing off the walls, rebounding into all ears. All ears, that is, with the obvious exception of Howie's. She kept it up, dauntlessly calling out to him: "I need that second cart now, Howie. *NOW.*" She rounded the corner in front of me, a disheveled young woman with a slurpy-faced baby in the basket of the cart and another child due, if I were any judge, in about three months. The woman looked bone weary. Her age was anywhere between twenty-five and forty. Her eyes were absolutely haunted.

Howie rounded the corner a-hummin' and knocked over a display of crackers at the end of the row. He had enough sense to stop and try to look abashed. It was a feeble attempt and a look obviously unfamiliar to his repertoire, because he succeeded only in looking as guilty as he was. Howie's poor mother bent to help him pick up the boxes, which had scattered in all directions. For a woman who had probably not seen her toes for weeks, she maneuvered gracefully.

I went to help, not Howie, but his mother. She gave me a smile so filled with gratitude I nearly cried. Did her husband appreciate her? He was apparently attracted to her, but that certainly wasn't enough.

The crackers started to look good, so I dropped a box into my basket. As I continued to help the woman, I tried to figure out why I had such an aversion to her son. He was, after all, just a little boy with energy. Howie looked no older than four. Some would say I had a premonition, an *inkling*, that somehow Howie would be the instrument of my demise. Perhaps. I've not thought about it. It no longer matters.

I *am* sure about one thing. I was stupid as well as unlucky (death can be unlucky as well as inconvenient). I did what my children repeatedly told me not to do (some switch, huh?) and climbed onto the lower shelves to reach the fabric softener way at the back of the top shelf. Grocery store shelves should not be that high or that deep. (If Ian had come along with me as he had offered, he would simply have reached up, taken down the bottle, and placed it into the basket.)

Okay, so there I was with one carefully placed foot stuck between two large detergent jugs on the bottom shelf as my left hand clung precariously to the tiny little metal edge of the top shelf. As I reached for the handle of the elusive fabric softener, **IT** happened. **IT** happened so quickly I was surprised to wake up dead, when I'd expected only minor injuries and some ugly bruises.

My foot slipped at the same time my fingernail, the mainstay of my grip on the top shelf, broke; my chin clanked into the middle shelf on my speedy way down; and I fell backward into the aisle.

Timing *is* everything. As this happened, Howie had again escaped from under the watchful eye of his mother; he and the fully laden grocery cart rounded the corner a-zinging, totally out of control. By the time my head hit the floor, Howie was unable to stop and the heavy cart careened into my right temple with a sickening thunk.

I was dead on the spot.

I woke up here in Heaven.

CHAPTER 3

"Crap! One more old lady smiles at me and tells me what a wonderful, loverly day this is, I just might sock her one in her saggin' boobs!"

That morning Juan had awaken in a foul mood, which had rapidly disintegrated as the day progressed. None of the Hellraisers were in a good mood. They were almost broke. Their collective financial worth was in the vicinity of three hundred dollars. This was not good, considering the expensive drug habits they so feverishly tried to support. The liquor they used to wash it down and get it humming through their narrowing veins wasn't cheap. No, not only were they broke and miserable, but they were also sober, a condition that brought out the worst in them and created mayhem for anyone misfortunate enough to be in their vicinity.

They were at their usual meeting spot under an overpass to Route 95 near the Delaware River. Cars and trucks rumbled over their heads, most exceeding the 55 mph speed limit and spewing exhaust fumes, which drifted downward to the gang's lair. The occasional screech of brakes echoed against the concrete abutments. Graffiti decorated the walls of their "office." Roger had some do-nuts he had stolen from Old Man Kelly's shop a few blocks south. Old Kelly never locked the back door to his bakery, so theft was pathetically easy. Roger liked more of a challenge, but he also was addicted, along with cocaine and alcohol, to donuts. He wasn't always so anxious to share his hard habits, but whenever he visited his donut source he brought a couple of dozen along for the gang.

"We gotta do sumpthin' an' we gotta do it *today!*" Juan slammed his right fist into the filthy palm of his left hand for emphasis, looking each of the gang members in the eye. "This shit hasta stop. I'm sick an' tired of havin' no dough."

Roger, the only one with a hint of a sense of humor, quite literally took his life into his hands and interrupted Juan by waving his donut in the air. "Yo! We got dough right here, man!" One of the others snickered softly, but it was hard to discover which one.

Juan momentarily glared at Roger, whose smile faded as fast as it had arrived. He bent his head to the task of eating his donut and dared not speak again while Juan held court.

"Have I told you yet today just how much of an asshole you are, Roger? No wonder you like donuts so much, they're just rolls with assholes in 'em. As I was sayin' when I was so rudely interrupted," he was still staring at Roger, "we gotta get out there today and get us a stash of cash." He stood up to underscore the urgency of his statement. All eyes were on him, not out of respect, but fear. If you could see Juan and what he was doing, you had a better chance of survival; defense was the key with this bunch of lowlifes.

"So, where ya want us t' go, then?" asked little Mike, some chocolate from his donut clung to the left corner of his mouth, making him look even more the child than his fourteen years. One glance into his eyes, however, and you immediately had the feeling that here was an "old" kid who knew his way around places many folks never even added for spice to their nightmares.

"We're gonna hit the tourists over near the stupid cracked bell and we're gonna get 'em good! As so many of the schmucks around here keep sayin', it *is* a wonderful day in the neighborhood, a perfect day for takin' us what we need from those who have so much to give. Hell, all they hafta do is call their bank and they send 'em more money, just like that. They'd feel great to know how they're helpin' the underprivileged Hellraisers!" Juan's laugh was a mean-sounding thing, more like a predatory growl than anything remotely associated with mirth or joy.

"When ya wanna start the fun?" Chun asked around a mouth full of donut, raspberry jelly oozed from his mouth like blood and dripped down his smooth chin. He privately despaired that he would never grow a beard.

"Let's go now!" Otis stood, wiping his greasy hands on even greasier and ragged jeans.

"Sit down, fool!" Juan barked. Otis sat. "We go when *I* say so, and not a minute before. You got it?" He didn't even wait for a response, but continued his instructions. "We gotta give the lovely people time to get their designer tourist clothes on, get the money sorted out in those soft leather wallets we want, and line up their little kiddies after breakfast on the vee-ran-dah. I say we head over to Independence Mall in about a hour." He stood up, a sure sign the others could now do the same without undue stress. They all stood, but made no move to leave until so bid.

"Now, guys, let's make ourselves proud. Let's get us as much as we can today. Doan take any extra risks. Doan call attention to yourself, kinda blend, you know? And, for shit's sake, keep your eyeballs open for the cops! Be back on this spot at six o'clock on the dot. Unnerstan'?"

His audience nodded in unison.

"Outta here! Happy huntin'!"

As the gang turned to leave, Juan reached out and roughly grabbed Roger by the shoulder. "Leave the girlies alone, Roger. I doan wanna hafta tell youse again. Got it?"

Roger nodded slowly.

"Good." Juan released Roger's shoulder with a strong shove.

✳✳✳

It was such a beautiful day that Emma was wide awake on her corner by the Public Ledger Building. It was a day that brought with it memories of other spring days, days that Emma could dimly remember, days that had been filled with joy and eager anticipation, days when her bones didn't ache, when she was warm and clean. It made her smile to remember what little she could bring out of the fog in her head. And it made her cry to remember. As she glanced around, she could see some bright orange school buses as they entered the large parking area across Market Street to disgorge the children, while teachers vainly tried to herd their charges into some sort of order. The children hopped and skipped around like little dervishes. This always made Emma smile.

As more people began to enter the Independence Mall area, Emma's hand perceptively tightened on the handle of her shopping bag. She had already checked her treasure several times. The ring still hung safely within the confines of the bag.

Emma leaned back against the red brick wall, which was still cool from the chill of the previous night. It was such fun to watch the children, and today promised to be especially filled with them, considering how early the first buses had arrived. Emma smiled again and sighed. She would have to go over to Washington Square Park in the afternoon, because Mister would expect her to leave the corner to him by then, but she would enjoy herself for now.

A sense of rightness and beauty pervaded the area of Independence Mall that morning. That would soon change—abruptly.

CHAPTER 4

When I first arrived in Heaven, I spent entire days lying on my soft, comfy cloudlette carpet enrapt in my Earth Views Receiver (EVR). I channel-hopped constantly, an activity that had annoyed me on Earth, whenever anyone did it. But here in Heaven, I surfed and I wept. I laughed. I muttered to myself in astonishment at how devotedly silly some of my family and friends were behaving. I was frustrated. I hollered at the huge screen as if I could make them hear me, listen to me, help them. I was angry. I was sorry for myself. I was a wreck.

And somewhere not long after I arrived, like maybe three days, I got it into my scrambled mind that there was one eeny, weeny, teensie little thing that could stand in the way of my complete Heavenly bliss—*Thelma*. Ian's wife. The Perfect Person. Granted, Ian had never once said Thelma was perfect, but she died when she was only thirty-four in a car accident that had, miraculously, spared their year-old son. She died before a wrinkle or gray hair could manifest themselves; before her body had time to reap the effects of gravity; before anything began to droop, sag, or downright disappear. They'd been married only three years when she died. That, alone, can rank a spouse pretty close to the pinnacle of a pedestal.

As I walked, I had my tasteful Heaven street map under my arm. I had located Thelma's cloudlette on the map the previous evening. It turned out she did not live far from me. It was time to make that visit. I had no idea what to expect, either from her or from me, for that matter.

Thelma was at home, getting ready to attend a Guardian Angel general meeting. She welcomed me with genuine warmth and graciousness. Begrudgingly, I could see much of what had attracted Ian all those years ago. She was not only charming and without guile, she was also adorable—not beautiful, thank whatever—but totally winsome. I hadn't had to introduce myself, which is not surprising when you realize Thelma, too, has an Earth Views Receiver. (Exactly *what* had she observed? Ohmygosh!)

"Debarelle! Or may I call you Rellie?"

I nodded and smiled.

"I am so happy to meet you!" She extended a welcoming, well-manicured hand in my direction.

"Thank you, Thelma." I took her hand, and as I did so, felt a great warmth of instant friendship. I certainly hadn't expected that from this source, let me tell you. I was learning that wondrous, amazing things happen here in Heaven every day.

"Please, sit down. I must apologize, but I have a meeting of Guardian Angels in a little less than an hour. Hey!" She executed a perfect half-pivot on one heel. "Why don't you come along with me? You're almost to Acceptance as it is (how could she know that?) and because it's a general meeting, you're welcome to sit in with a member. It could help in your decision, once you're an Angel. Will you come with me?"

Damnit, but she was nice. *Perfectly* nice. I found myself agreeing to go along, after we had some tea. We don't need to eat or drink here, but we can if we want to. Most N.A.s (Newly Arrived) want to because you can eat and drink anything at all, as much as you want, as long as you want and never, ever have to count nasty things like calories or cholesterol. As with many a novelty, this soon wears off, but there is the occasional partaking. A nice, friendly tea can be just the thing.

Once we were settled, teacups balanced in time-worn fashion, Thelma said, "You know, Rellie, I was rooting for you and was so glad to see Agatha left in the dust, casseroles and all." She giggled prettily.

Speechlessness is not one of my strong suits, but she thoroughly floored me. My face froze somewhere between a smile and a grimace; I was afraid to blink my eyes. My brain was totally nonfunctional. I did the only thing I could do … nothing.

She continued. "I know how you must feel, Rellie, truly I do. I felt much the same way when I first got here at a much younger death-age. I'd only begun to live, I thought. I'd had to leave a terrific husband, as you know, and a wonderful little boy. Acceptance was very long and hard in coming to me and that's The Truth." She smiled and took a sip of her tea, eyeing me over the edge of the cup.

My power of speech returned, thank goodness. I inched into the conversation with a real smile and said, "I'm beginning to see how difficult that was. I mean, I've been super-pissed that I had to leave my family, but I had the added joy of grandkids and great-grandkids as well as," I took a deep breath and plunged, "finally meeting a man I could love and who, I believe, loved me, all in the same relationship."

"Ian." His name was stated simply and softly.

"Yes, Ian. Come to think of it, we both knew him about the same length of time, you just a bit longer, perhaps, and each of us at a different point in her life, and his."

"Yes, it's as if he were a different person to both of us, isn't it?" she asked. "I suppose, in actuality, he was different, don't you think? And yet the same, too?"

She had just given me a dose of cogitating material.

"There's so much more to discuss, but we'd better hurry to the meeting. You will come with me, won't you?" She stood to take the empty cup from my hand.

Handing her the cup, I found I was anxious to accompany her to the meeting. "I'd like that. Thanks."

It was as we walked to the meeting that I felt most strongly I was being observed. It was odd. Thelma rattled on pleasantly about the various sites we were passing, talking about different people and so on, oblivious to what was happening to me. What was happening to me was an increasing feeling of paranoia. I started looking over my shoulder at each little turn of the road, and Heavenly roads turn constantly. It wouldn't do to have a road sing through someone's cloudlette.

"Don't look now, Thelma, but … I said, don't look *now!*" She had, of course, immediately turned around. No wonder Lot's wife got herself salted. She would have been fine if left alone, but no, Lot had to go and say, "Dear, you are forbidden to look back because something awful will happen if you do. So do me a little favor and don't turn around." (Lot, in the way of men, had totally forgotten the little altercation they'd had over the camel bill just that morning, when he'd accused her of not getting the payment out in time. He had let it be known it was her fault if the camel were repossessed. He'd said something like "the apple didn't fall far from the tree" in reference to her mother. Naturally, after all of that domestic hodgepodge, Mrs. Lot was not about to listen to one more word her husband had to say. He was not going to tell her what she could and could not do. The rest, as the saying goes, is history. Although, I'm not sure what happened to the camel.)

"Oh, sorry!" Thelma said, obviously amused and not really sorry at all. "What was back there? There's nothing there now."

"Of course not!" I said, a bit put off. "Has anyone ever been mugged in Heaven?" I turned to look once again. I could have sworn I saw a tall shadow move.

After laughing for what seemed like ten minutes with pure mirth and joy, and causing no small amount of stares from passersby, Thelma was able to control herself sufficiently to gasp, "Good Heavens, no!" before riding the tide of laughter again, holding her sides and wiping tears from her cheeks.

I continued doggedly. "You can't tell me there aren't any reformed or repentant muggers here. Maybe one of them has slipped a bit and should be checked or whatever, reviewed. I know there are periodic reviews for marginal cases. Which reminds me, I wanted to mention my first husband ..."

"He was a *mugger?* I never caught that." Thelma was scandalized.

"No, Thelma, Charles was a *bugger*. There must be something wrong out there at one of the gates, because he got in." I was actually wringing my hands. Lady Macbeth couldn't have done it any better.

"Oh, that. Just because you didn't like him doesn't mean there were no redeeming qualities, you know."

"They were the best hidden qualities in the world," I growled.

"Now, your second husband, the Board just could not justify his admittance in the slightest. You were smart to stay with him for only seven months. You acted perfectly right after he hit you. That dentist did an excellent job, by the way." (Was there anything they didn't know about you here?) "I think," she continued, "you are being followed, too."

I spun around to look behind me. Nothing. "You do? Have you seen someone? Who is it? Why are they following me? What can we do about it? When ..."

She put her hand softly on my arm, and we stopped right there in the middle of the road. "There are a lot of nice surprises up here. Give them time; they'll come. I think it's your G.A."

"My *what?*"

"Sorry. Your Guardian Angel, G.A. for short."

"I still have a Guardian Angel?" Right on the heels of this thought, "If it is my G.A., I've got a few things to say to him or her. It wouldn't have been that difficult to let me at the fabric softener, would it? Where is he? I'll bet he's afraid to show his face the way he's skulking around." I glanced behind us again before we started walking. Still nothing, no one was there.

Thelma wisely said no more on the subject, and we were soon in front of the Guardian Angel Auditorium. It was crowded with G.A.s and angels drifting around, talking to each other. A few N.A.s (like me) were in the tow of other G.A.s (like Thelma). I waved, recognizing some of the others who had arrived when I did.

"Him." Thelma said, as we waited.

"What?"

"Your G.A. is a him, one of the most popular G.A.s here; he has fewer foul-ups than most."

"You could have fooled me. Have you seen some of the things that idiot let me do?" I was irritated. Where was that fool?

"No, but once you've reviewed his report of your case, you may understand a little better."

"His *what?*"

"Report. Didn't you know about that? What have you been doing up here for the past eight months? You should have gotten to that part of your study material by now. Oh, dear. It would really be a smart idea to get on with the Acceptance bit, you know."

We were climbing the stairs, heading for the beautifully carved wood doors. Each door was inlaid with stained glass and trimmed in what appeared to be gold. Heaven sure has terrific standards. I was definitely born for this. Well…

"What's this report thing, Thelma?"

"His name is Etienne," she said.

Were we having the same conversation? Must be, no one else was nearby.

"Who?"

"Your G.A."

"Oh. And the report?"

"Rellie, reports aren't named!" she said and raised one eyebrow at me before smiling.

"Of course not," I said and smiled back.

"Good." She looked perplexed. What was wrong with her?

"What report were you talking about my reviewing to help me understand the goof-up Etienne?" Grammatically, that question could have used some polishing, but I was impatient, to say the least.

Tender Thelma, no wonder she came up here early; Earth would've killed her. Well, come to think of it, it did. She proceeded to explain how every N.A., with no exceptions, once Acceptance was achieved and Angel status is assured, was given by the Acceptance Committee a detailed report written by the person's guardian angel. It encompassed the entire life, from the moment of birth through the moment of death, sparing nothing between. The G.A. offered explanations for every job completed on the person's behalf. The N.A. has the right to question his or her G.A. in depth. This report is essential to the G.A. and his rating with the Guardian Angel Committee and will show if he needs to go for a refresher or can begin another guard duty immediately. That did it! Etienne was going to go hoarse explaining. Just wait till I got hold of him.

"Does it include some of the more uncomfortable or painful parts of a life?" I wanted to know.

"Yes, it does. It's the complete life. It must all be reviewed and understood before you can move on," she told me. "It is often quite humorous, you'll see," she added with a smile. "What wasn't particularly funny on Earth, is often perceived differently here."

"You want humorous, wait outside after I read that report. You may have to stop me from harming Etienne," I told her as we entered the auditorium.

"You may be spared his presence for much longer, Rellie. I've heard some rumors that Etienne has chosen, instead, to be reborn this time."

"Humpfh! How soon can the coward go?"

I think Thelma smiled again before she turned her head.

CHAPTER 5

The lavishly appointed lobby was bursting at the seams with angels, G.A.s, and a few lucky N.A.s like me. Music surrounded us; it came from a sound system that would be the envy of any radio personality or band leader on Earth. Comfortable blue and mauve upholstered wing chairs were everywhere.

Everybody seemed to know Thelma. After all, she'd been here for a long time. We stopped every few feet to talk and for me to be introduced. When we finally sat, just before the lights dimmed three times to let us know the meeting would soon be coming to order, I realized I had not been bored for one single, solitary little second since meeting Thelma that morning. What's more, I was actually enjoying myself. I'd obviously spent too much time alone on my cloudlette with my face in the Earth Views Receiver. How masochistic I'd been. Maybe I really was on my way to Acceptance with a capital "A."

As soon as everyone was seated, the President G.A. rang a beautiful crystal bell. The meeting officially began with a rousing *á cappella* chorus of "Guardian Angels Together," sung to the tune I recognized as The Doors's "Light My Fire." I found it a curious choice on which to base a Heavenly song, but there it was. Not yet knowing the words, I was nevertheless caught up in the spirit of it and hummed along, verse after verse after verse. Our collective voices reverberated around the immense auditorium. It was not at all like services at my former church, where a few people sang while others tried to wake up, or sober up, or even stand up on a Sunday morning. No, these angels let it all rip and *SANG!*

There was no need for a Treasurer's report. We moved right along to the Secretary's report of the previous meeting. As he read his report, I discovered Heaven was a truly busy place, administered carefully and not at all the passive place of ephemeralness I had expected, when I had considered it at all, that is. I was so in awe of the place and in what I was hearing, that I missed some of the items discussed.

I found the meeting a fantastic experience, nothing at all like the remembered and interminably boring meetings of boards, committees, and panels from my past. During the break, Thelma and I got up to walk around, to mix with the group. By then, I was beginning to recognize some of the folks I'd met outside. And I continued to feel I was being watched.

A large female angel, brown hair in whispy curls all around her narrow face, rushed over to us. "Oh!" she gasped, "Aren't you just alive with excitement?" Her metaphor was interesting. Her hands fluttered in the air like birds caught in a downdraft.

"Yes." Thelma replied in a tone that seemed, for all the world, as if she knew what this other angel was talking about. Perhaps the hands were saying something I wasn't hearing, like hula dance communication. Thelma continued, "It should be the highlight of many meetings to come." She turned to me, "You are very lucky to be here for this, Rellie," she said as if that would clear up the whole thing.

I'd heard that the instructions for dealing with idiots, persons with very high fevers, small children, drunks, and various political aspirants are to do nothing except to smile.

I smiled.

"Our guest speaker, Rellie. That's what we're talking about," Thelma clarified, possibly after looking into my face and seeing the confusion there. "Saint Peter is the keynote speaker here today! Getting him is almost impossible these days, what with gate crashers and the increased volume of arrivals. Wait till the bulk of those Baby Boomers starts to arrive, it'll be a circus around here. You'll love Saint Peter, Rellie. He has the most terrific voice and is a real sweetheart. I've got to deliver this envelope," she waved a small manila envelope in the air. "I'll meet you back at our seats. Circulate. Go over and say hello to Etienne." She waved the envelope in the direction of the far northern corner of the lobby and was gone.

Etienne? Did I dare meet him now? Could I control myself in public? How would I know him? Ridiculous. Deciding to circulate in a casual manner, I strolled slowly around the sides of the room, observing as much as I could.

"Hi!" A friendly voice spoke near my left shoulder.

I turned around to find myself facing a pleasing and smiling face, just as so many were around here. "Hi!" I returned the smile.

"You must be Scott's mother; he looks so much like you!" enthused this man.

"Yes, I am." My pride caused me to stand up taller.

"He sure was a handful when he was little, wasn't he? It's a wonder we survived," said the fellow.

I could offer only a blank stare, a blink.

"I'm Carstairs, Scott's G.A., and I'm pleased to meet you," he proffered a large hand. The word *paw* came to mind.

I shook his hand, an automatic reflexive action, and demanded, "Where in the world were you when Scott fell and broke his back and was nearly paralyzed? Where were you when he got lost in Chicago at the train depot and we were all so frantically looking for him that we missed our train home? And, for Heaven's sake, just where in the name of goodness were you when he had his first broken heart and nearly went crazy, *did* go crazy for a while? Huh, where the hell *were* you?" If this is the way I was talking to my son's guardian angel, Etienne had better move out, get reborn, go somewhere fast.

Carstairs had the grace to look nonplused.

"I'm so sorry, where are my manners," I said, recovering somewhat. "I ..."

"That's perfectly all right," said Carstairs. "Many persons react in this manner, especially mother persons. I try never to be a G.A. for someone who will eventually become a mother, too taxing for one's emotions, don't you see?" He smiled again.

I re-evaluated my original opinion of him. Anyone who could still smile like that and be my son's G.A. deserved all the kindness one was capable of giving. I was about to say something more, most likely in the way of an apology, when I heard my name being called. "Rellie! Oh, Rellie!" I saw Thelma coming through the crowd like a hot knife through margarine, towing a rather bemused-looking man.

Carstairs took a quick look in their direction and mumbled, "Uh, oh!" and beat a fast retreat. I wondered why he did that, but not for long.

The two arrived before me, none the worse for wear. Again, I smiled and waited. Whoever this person with Thelma was, he was as handsome a man as I'd seen in a long, long time. If orders could be taken, he was what I would have ordered: tall, well over six feet; bearded with sparkling brown eyes and humor lines all over his face; and, as I was about to find out, a warm and gentle voice. If there was a brain and sensitivity inside the package, well, perfection really can be achieved. Ian who?

"Rellie, this is Etienne." Thelma said and left us. She did not beat around bushes. She did, however, beat a neat retreat in the same direction Carstairs had taken.

Etienne. *The* Etienne? The screw-up? The fool? My G.A.? The insensitive lout? This magnificent creature was *Etienne*? Oh, drat. Someone must have made a mistake. Thelma was joking. It was a dream; I must have dozed off standing next to Carstairs. Maybe this guy had lied and he's pretending to be

Etienne for some reason known only to him and Thelma. Etienne
hired this person to check my reaction out first? Dadgum it!

"Hello, Debarelle," the most wonderful voice I'd ever heard
say my name had spoken. "I'm Etienne, your former, well, not
quite yet former, Guardian Angel, and before you clobber me, I
want you to know I love you."

It was said with such simplicity and sincerity that I could have
fainted had I not been so rigid with anger. So this was Etienne.
What an abysmal shame. I wanted to do two things at once: knock
the living daylights out of him and drag him off to the nearest
cloudlette to stay forever. I recovered quickly, remembering the
ineptitude of the fool. I mean, how could he have let me experience so much pain and sorrow when he claimed to love me? Some
love that was.

There he stood, just smiling at me. He could have no idea
what thoughts were raging around my head or he would have run
for the hills. I opened my mouth to deliver my Where Were You
When speech, the one I'd just tried out on Carstairs, but with a
bit more punch and definitely longer and more vehement, when
another G.A. came dashing up to us, eyes wide as saucers, and
totally out of breath.

"Etienne! There you are, I've been looking all over for you!"
he exclaimed, with what little puff of breath he had left. He was
literally hopping up and down, when he noticed me for the first
time. He paused to catch his breath and nodded briefly in the
direction of my right elbow.

I smiled. I'd been doing a lot of that lately. This time, for
variety's sake, I added what I considered a friendly nod.

"Calm down, Wilbur," Etienne said, gently laying a hand on
Wilbur's arm. "Take a moment to get your breath and then tell
me what's going on." He dropped his hand and motioned Wilbur
over to the side of the room, raising an eyebrow at me as if to say,
"Are you coming?"

Whoooooa! Forget that stuff, mister! I took a step toward the auditorium, when I heard Wilbur say, "She's in labor, Etienne, your new mother just went into labor. It's her second. As you know, you'll have an older brother, so it won't take her long to birth you, lucky you. The whole process is tough on the head, especially the nose and ears. I'm always afraid I'll get an ear torn off or my nose will be pushed to the middle of my forehead. That would scare them, wouldn't it? And I'm never quite sure what to do with my arms. I did not enjoy that whole process and have avoided reborning for quite a while. But *you* have to get to the Reborning Platform right away!" Wilbur said, as he resumed his hopping.

Curiosity had me firmly within its grip, so I decided to follow the raised eyebrow. Dreams can really come true here in Heaven and at a rapid rate. I had wished it, and now Etienne was actually going away to be reborn. If there is any justice at all, even one tiny little shred of it, maybe I could become *his* Guardian Angel. Oh, but the thought sustained me; it actually gave me chills, tingles, and flutters. I'd found my incentive to work on Acceptance.

"Debarelle ... Rellie?" Etienne began, his gorgeous eyes filling his handsome face. Could he actually want me to throw my arms around him and plead, with a tearful voice, for him not to go? If I had the time, hell, I'd help him pack. I'd take his arm, lead him to that platform and stay with him until he left with the stork or however he got from here to that womb. I'd wave. I'd smile. I'd sigh with profound relief.

At that moment, the lights flickered on and off to indicate that Saint Peter would be speaking as soon as we were seated. "I have to get back to my seat. Have a good trip," I said magnanimously, secure in the knowledge that he was leaving. Was that what one said to someone embarking on rebirth? Well, that's what I said.

I walked away quickly, leaving Etienne and Wilbur to their plans and headed into the auditorium. Thelma was already in her seat; I sat beside her as the lights dimmed.

"Nice maneuver, Thelma-girl," I whispered; it sounded more like a hiss. I doubted that is a good sound in Heaven.

"Oh, Rellie. He's so very nice and he loves you so," she whispered softly. "I'm a sucker for romance." Even where it doesn't exist?

"He's the sucker," I said and shrugged my shoulders. "But he's off to be reborn at this moment, thank goodness. My only question is: Who will review his report with me now?" I suddenly realized I wanted Etienne with me, so I could yell at him. He was getting off far too easily. He'd probably arranged it so he wouldn't have to be there with me. What a chicken.

When Thelma heard what I said, she nearly leaped from her seat as if I'd pinched her. "No! No! He *can't* be reborn, not now! No! Not *now!* Something must be done! She's early, much too early. He has to go over his report with you; he can't be reborn until that's done. Honestly, scheduling has gotten totally out of control around here. The Rebirth Schedulers used to leave a lot more leeway in the system to allow for N.A. Acceptance lead-times and report reviewing than they do now, and this is what can happen. We've got to do something!" She had herself totally worked up.

A few polite whispers of "Please, sit down" and "Down in front," convinced Thema that she should, indeed, sit and would have to deal with the situation later.

"Ladies and gentlemen, Saint Peter," the announcer said. There was no preamble; none was necessary for this guest. Saint Peter was greeted with thunderous applause; the walls echoed and the ceiling pulsed with it.

He entered from our left, crossed to the center of the stage, and stood before the podium. The applause grew, swelling to a feverish pitch. The audience was apparently too well bred to actually stomp its feet and whistle, but the noise level approached the painful.

Saint Peter stood, calm and assured, and looked out over the crowd. He slowly raised his right hand in greeting. The silence was immediate, like the turning off of a light switch that can turn a bright room into a place of dark serenity. The silence was palatable.

And still Saint Peter stood glancing out over the audience, making each one of us feel we were the one at whom he looked with such warmth and intensity. I felt naked before him, but not at all nervous. This fellow knew all about me anyhow—and he had still let me in. You can't hide stuff in this place. They know all about you by the time you reach the outside of The Gates. They are the ones who decide whether or not to open those gates and let you in.

Saint Peter was not unusually tall. We seem to imagine someone who is prominent or famous as being tall, large in stature, to match our awareness of his or her notability. Saint Peter was not tall, but neither was he short, just a pleasing in-between. His eyes and his hair were neither dark nor light. He was neither thin nor heavy. He was not someone you would look at twice, if you passed him on the street. Ah, but when he spoke, there was the difference, the magic, the marvel!

I'd only heard him say "Welcome to Heaven, Debarelle. It is so good to have you here with us" on the afternoon I'd arrived. To be honest, I was so nervous and pissed that afternoon, that I hadn't paid too much attention to him. I remember feeling a bit of relief that The Gates had actually opened to me. Because I needed to reside somewhere in my condition, this place had the other options beat by miles.

We were all, each and every one of us, held enthralled by this man's voice. He could have read the ingredients on a tomato sauce label for all I cared. His voice caressed us. There was nowhere else in Heaven I wanted to be than right there in the auditorium. I do not remember to this day precisely what Saint Peter spoke about that first time I heard him. I remember only his tone, his delivery, and his presence. He did call for more care on the part of G.A.s, and he pushed for specialization amongst G.A.s, something I'd not known existed. It seems G.A.s can share particularly difficult cases and challenging crises, a fact that would prove pertinent in my existence very soon.

Saint Peter did not speak for long. In fact, he was the first keynote speaker that ever, in my knowledge, left his audience wanting *more*. He left the stage in the same quiet, dignified manner in which he had arrived. His departure was to the same thunderous applause. Saint Peter is well loved here in Heaven.

During a slight break in the agenda, I turned to Thelma and said, "Can you tell me exactly what I may have done to deserve Etienne as a G.A.?"

Thelma had lifted off from reality. "Hmmmm?" came her dreamy response. "Oh." Touch down. "Just lucky, I guess."

My fingers felt as if they were turning into talons; I could feel the change. I would not have been surprised if claws sprouted from the ends of my fingers at any moment. I would then jump out of the seat, a raging Valkyrie. I didn't doubt for one iota of a second that I would attack Etienne.

"Thelma!" It was my call for help.

"I'm sorry, Rellie, really I am." She giggled.

"Umpfh!" More would have been too much of an effort for me. A smile was out of the question this time.

When I was sure I was losing it, Thelma put her hand gently on my wrist. Had she sensed I was contemplating a hurtle? "Rellie, Etienne may not often be able at first try to remember his left from his right, but he always, and I mean *always*, has his heart in the right place. Remember that, please."

Some of the tension passed out of my body. She must have sensed this as well, because she removed her hand from my wrist. I felt somewhat ashamed. I was still angry with Etienne, but I should have retained my sense of justice. Maybe that hadn't come along for the ride. My Earthly life had been longer than many and over-flowed with joy and happiness, dwelling on the inevitable miseries of living would do no one any good, certainly not now. Besides, look where I was! Bliss City. Etienne still had a lot of accounting to do, however, I no longer wanted to banish him to the back of beyond forever, just *almost* forever.

The meeting continued, but my mind was elsewhere. How *could* Etienne be so inept but look like the angel he literally was?

It seemed like only minutes since the meeting had begun, when it was adjourned with another exuberant singing of "Guardian Angels Together." For those who chose to partake, milk, honey, and ambrosia were served in the upper lobby.

CHAPTER 6

By the time the school buses had parked in the lot north of Market Street in Philadelphia, Rissa and her best friend, Jamie, had an itinerary written on the back of Jamie's left hand.

"Read it to me," Rissa said, "so I can see if it makes any sense." She hopped down the steps of the bus, landed on the cracked macadam, and followed Jamie to a shaded area behind the bus, away from most of the teachers. In spite of a lovely spring breeze, it felt a bit cool and Rissa rubbed her arms to warm up.

"Okay, here we go," Jamie stood taller and lowered her voice dramatically. "First, we might as well go check out the Bell, because it's right over there," she pointed toward its place of display. "What's that sheet Teach gave us say about it?"

Rissa had stuffed the paper into her back jeans pocket and went through several interesting gyrations and swivels to remove the now very wrinkled paper. One of the boys bouncing off the bus whistled at her. She ignored him and smoothed out the paper between her hands and read: "The Liberty Bell is housed … blah, blah, blah … it first rang to announce the signing of the Declaration of Independence … was made in England in 1752 … cracked soon after arriving in Philadelphia … was recast but cracked for good when it was tolling for the funeral of Chief Justice John Marshall in 1835 … symbol of America's freedom … that's enough. Guess we should take a look at it. It's close, so maybe we could save time for Tower Records." Rissa folded the paper once more, but held on to it. "Hand me your hand, Jamie. Let's see what else you've got on hand for us. Oh, such great puns!" Her laughter was sweet and blended with Jamie's mock groan of disgust.

"Ohhhhh, god! Rissa that was terrible," Jamie grimaced, while proffering her hand as if it were to be kissed by a gallant squire. "Read on, oh punny one," she giggled.

"Independence Hall," she opened the paper in her hand and continued, after casually tossing her pigtail from her shoulder so it hung down the middle of her back. "Independence Hall, once called the Pennsylvania State House, is where the final draft of the Declaration of Independence was adopted on July 4, 1776 ..."

"Ta, dah! This is why we have fireworks and barbecues!" said Jamie with a small hop of joy.

"Good grief. To continue in an obviously vain attempt to educate you, this was also where the Constitution was written and signed. Jamie?" Rissa knew the moment she looked up that Jamie, although physically standing not less that three feet from her, was "off" somewhere. "JAMIE!" Rissa increased the volume of her voice.

"The cutest guy just walked by, Rissa. I think we should go to see the Liberty Bell right now!" She tugged at Rissa's sleeve. "He's headed that way!" Jamie pointed in the appropriate direction. The direction she wanted to go. The direction she wanted to go NOW.

Rissa, long used to such behavior from Jamie, who was nothing if not consistent, shoved the descriptions back into the back pocket of her jeans and followed her friend, as the teacher called after the rapidly dispersing group: "Stay in this area, no wandering off. Keep together. It's eleven-thirty now. We'll meet back here at bus fourteen no later than three o'clock."

***

The "cute" guy was none other than Juan on his second scouting mission. He had already ascertained that the area was, indeed, ripe with 'rich bitch' tourists. An entire busload of Asian tourists had recently arrived; a camera swung from each and every neck. It would be a cinch to snip and clip the cameras from the straps and pawning them would be a breeze.

But Chun would hear nothing of it. "Cameras!" he snorted derisively. "Hell, man. We want *money*. Why bother with cameras that we have to pawn, when we can go right for the cash?"

Juan supposed Chun had a point, because many of the expensive cameras could be traced, but he also felt Chun was being race protective and he wouldn't tolerate that from any of the Hellraisers. You took from anybody, a mark was a mark, plain and simple.

Juan was making his second pass of the area when he saw Jamie pull Rissa across Market Street, directly in front of a horse-drawn carriage. The horse stopped suddenly, roughly jerking the passengers in their seats. Juan smiled. Stupid tourists deserved it, spending good money to ride behind a sissy horse wearing a shit bag under its tail. Couldn't let the tourists step in anything and ruin their Guccis. What a crock! The girls were cute. He looked again. Yep, she was definitely primo stuff, especially the ditzy one with the bouncy red curls, the one pulling the taller one with the pigtail. Two nice butts. He paused to watch them, no sense in wasting perfectly good scenery. It sure had the historical crap beat.

Meanwhile, Roger was slinking around the side of Congress Hall on Sixth Street near the corner at Chestnut Street. He, too, was watching all of the girls pass by. He remembered promising Juan he would leave them alone, but there was no harm in watching them, was there? He had a constant urge to touch girls, but right now he was here for another reason, and that was to get money from the tourists, so he'd just look for now. His eyes focused on Rissa's bouncing pigtail. He was unaware that he was drooling.

Chun, Mike, and Otis were busy bumping into people, removing their wallets and purses with practiced ease, before running away. It was more fun than football and they enjoyed the entire process. They had it worked out as slick as a machine. Chun would bump, excuse himself to the person, thereby distracting him or her, while Otis bumped again and lifted a wallet or a purse. Otis quickly passed the goods to Mike, who was nearby in the crowd, and who could outrun a gazelle. By the time Chun and Otis met up with Mike a few blocks away, Mike would have extracted the money and disposed of the wallets and purses. They often wondered why people worked when this was so rewarding and easy. Dum schmucks.

***

Because it was a beautiful day, the area swarmed with people out to enjoy it. Emma continued to sit against the building, the metal plaque at the corner of the wall proclaiming "Public Ledger Building" for all who cared to know. It would soon be time for the Changing of the Guard, and Emma was feeling a bit concerned this day. While Roger, Juan, and the others watched the tourists, Emma watched them. She knew they were Bad Ones and kept a close eye on their activities, lest they should somehow threaten her. So far they had kept away from her, but storms brewed quickly on the streets and Emma was wise in her caution. She did not feel threatened yet; if she did, she would move on to Washington Square Park, although it would mean missing the Changing of the Guard and Mister. She didn't want to admit it to herself, but she looked forward to seeing Mister every day, his was a friendly face in a sea of noncommittal and harsh ones. But she was a survivor and would not knowingly put herself in the path of the Bad Ones.

She sat watching as Juan slithered among the tourists. She saw Roger oogling the girls and actually drooling. She knew the tricks of Chun, Otis, and Mike. She knew all about the Bad Ones. And she kept her peace. If the tourists were not smart enough to hang on to what they had, it wasn't her place to become involved. It was tough enough fending for herself, finding enough newspapers to keep warm and finding food. She sometimes thought the pigeons in the parks had it a lot better than she did. People were always sitting on the nice benches at lunch hour and tossing food to the pigeons. Why didn't they let her have the half-sandwich they no longer wanted or the cookies that had crumbled in the plastic baggie? She wondered what those folks would think if she suddenly grabbed the food intended for the birds. They'd probably arrest her or put her in one of Those Places where crazy people wet their pants and mumbled at lamps. It was hard sometimes and she was often terribly hungry.

Emma sighed and smiled at herself. Silly old biddy. Why, she had her morning corner, Mister, her treasure, and friends over in the park. She was a lucky lady in this miserable world. Nonetheless, she continued to keep her eyes on the Bad Ones.

CHAPTER 7

I spent an inordinate amount of time staring into my EVR the night after the guardian angel meeting. I was inspired and wanted to fully Accept. I thought I might want to become a guardian angel and *do* something to save some poor living bugger the ignominious fate of having an Etienne-type G.A. I hadn't worked up to forgetting all of the nastiness Etienne had let me suffer, nor had I begun to inch toward forgiveness in that matter.

After the meeting, Thelma and I took a long walk before going to our homes. All in all, I was feeling comforted, excited, and content by the time I arrived back at my cloudlette. Heaven was looking up at last. High on the list of things that were responsible for my feelings, admittedly, was the fact that Etienne was probably being reborn that very night. I wished him a long, long life. I wondered who would really be his G.A., because I could not do the job at this stage in my progress.

Progress? *What* progress? I had been moping and emotionally Earth-bound ever since arriving. Today, I had taken a first step toward Acceptance by going out to meet others and attend that meeting. The fact that I thoroughly liked Thelma attested to some improvement in my attitude. I mean, she was once married to the man I had to leave behind and had been dreaming about seeing again when, in all likelihood, he would elect to be with her when he arrived. I noticed less sharpness in the pang I had previously felt at the thought.

In spite of all of this supposed "progress," I had decided earlier in the evening that perhaps the best way to reach Acceptance was to watch where I used to live. I tuned in to Earth. I was right. Real acceptance began that night.

I tuned in first to Sara, my beautiful daughter and mother of Marissa (Rissa), recently turned seventeen; Warren (Wren), eighteen; and Alexander, Jr. (Alex), twenty. Those kids were close in age yet miles apart in disposition. There had been a five-year stretch during which Sara seemed perennially pregnant, her stomach swelling and shrinking like a tide.

Sara stood, gorgeous and slim, at her kitchen sink concocting one of her masterpiece meals. I wondered anew how I could have given birth to this magnificent creature. Her husband, Alex, stood at the center island cutting the makings for a salad. I couldn't have ordered her a better husband, if I'd been given the job. Sara is a casting director for the city's fine arts theater and Alex is the vice president of a bank. They have regular hours and a fairly organized existence.

From the sounds echoing off the walls, I gathered Wren was in the general vicinity of his stereo system and Alex was as far away from it as possible, engrossed in his computer. Wren was muscle; Alex was brain. Rissa was energy and talent, gifted with a lovely singing voice. A total of six dogs lolled around the house, hardly a room free of one. They often joked about having a dog for each member of the family plus one for the dogs.

All seemed well at my daughter's household at the moment. I was not naive enough, however, to believe things would remain that way. I quickly switched to my son's household, where it is generally less structured and domestic. Unlike his sister, Scott has a "loose" schedule, very unstructured. He likes it that way, actually thrives on it. He is an air personality at WWOW, the major rock station in the city. Justine, his wife, is a chiropractor with an office attached to their home. She spends more time in the office than in the rest of the entire house. People manage to get out of whack at the oddest hours and insist on Justine putting them back together then and there. She is a good-hearted lady who doesn't tell them she sleeps or has any other life except to sit and wait for them to call.

I was pleasantly surprised to find them all at home, with the exception of my grandson, Robert (twenty) who was a junior in college and who still had not made up his mind what he wanted to do with his life "after Mom and Dad." My granddaughter, Jessica, and her husband, David, were visiting along with their sixteen-month old twins Tommy and Kami (a girl). I hadn't much time with them before I left … er … died. The time I did have wore me out, but they are adorable.

I left there quickly. I have learned that much by now: When things are good, get out.

Ian was next. I found him in his den, sitting in his favorite easy chair, a glass of red wine on the end table and a newspaper in his lap, as he listened to soft rock on the radio, his eyes closed. He looked totally relaxed. I smiled, turned off the EVR and, as I sank into my insanely soft couch, the realization finally reached my mind: I was *dead.* D-e-a-d. Dead to the Earth. But I was alive and well here in Heaven. I now felt I was well into the Acceptance phase. I could feel it. I had a present existence filled to the brim with marvels and friends, old and new. There would come a time when my Earth-living loved ones and I would meet again. Let them live, love, laugh, worry, and die as it was meant to be. It was time for me to move on, to let go of the past. Perhaps I would become a guardian angel. I could help *someone.* It was a goal, a purpose, and I was suddenly quite content.

A gentle knock at my front door interrupted my reverie. It was Thelma.

"What's going on? What's that grin all about?" she asked as soon as I opened the door and she got a look at my face. "Oh, I see you've Accepted. I'm so very happy for you!" She gave me a little squeeze.

"Yes, just *seconds* ago. Amazing place, Heaven. But, thanks. I'm glad, too." I returned her squeeze, then took her arm and led her to the couch. "Thelm, have a seat for a minute, would you? Can I ask you something?"

Thelma sat on the floor, a girl after my own heart. "Sure, Rellie. What?"

I joined her on the floor. "You weren't upset or hurt when I was with Ian, were you?" I was, once again, curious and somewhat paranoid.

"No, I wasn't. It was Etienne who helped me with that," she said.

"Etienne! Can't we just forget that fool? Must he show up in every conversation? What could he possibly have done that was not fouled up?"

"Rellie, he loves you. I know I keep saying that, but it's true. What he did was to point out that you deserved a little bit of happiness, *finally*, and Ian was giving that to you. And Etienne knew you would be here quite soon. An added bonus for me was that you made Ian very happy, Rellie. He deserved it, too."

I simply hugged her before our conversation turned to the more mundane. Our subsequent chat was accompanied by hot tea and warm scones with melted butter. It was sinfully delicious, considering where we are, but marvelous all the same.

After Thelma left, I was suddenly in a hurry to get on with Acceptance-required things. No sooner had I settled in with my handbook, study materials, and maps than I heard a soft sound at my cloudlette's entrance. I'd forgotten to close the door because the breeze was so pleasant. I turned to look. There stood Etienne. I stared at him. What was he doing *here*?

"I'm not going," he said quietly, his eyes boring into mine.

Be calm, Rellie. Count to five hundred and forty-seven million. "Why not? Why the hell not?" I didn't even try to keep the desperation out of my voice.

"May I come in, Rellie?"

If only he wasn't so damned (there I go again) handsome, so dingfuddled nice. If only he weren't so all-fired inept. If only he weren't my G.A. If only he weren't *here*. If only I knew for sure just what to do with him.

"Come in," I said, the manners my mother had instilled in me continued to thrive in spite of everything, "and have a seat. This I want to hear from the very beginning." I put my study materials aside.

"Studying?" He glanced around the room.

"Etienne, who was it who once said 'You have an amazing grasp of the obvious'?"

"Yeah ... well ..." He sat on the edge of the couch cushion, totally ill at ease. Tough.

"Get on with it, Etienne, please. Why aren't you the bouncing baby boy of some mush-headed couple who has no idea who they have?" I couldn't help it. He unnerves me.

He looked askance at me before, as was typical, not answering my question directly. I've never met anyone who so enjoyed swimming around issues as Etienne. "Did you ever wonder why I was being reborn and not continuing as a guardian angel?"

"No." (In fact, I had tried very hard not to think of you at all.)

"The fact of the matter is, I felt a need to take some time off from guarding. I was burnt out; I'd been doing it for quite a while. Besides, guarding you and loving you at the same time placed great stress on me, so I opted for rebirth." It was apparent he needed no reply from me. "Anyway, I was standing on the Reborning Platform awaiting my turn. I had chosen my new birth parents carefully, very carefully. When I chose, there was no doubt in my mind I had to go through with the new birth. As I stood there, I realized I didn't want to go yet, not just yet, not when you ... (he cleared his throat loudly) ... I was second in line when Carstairs came rushing up to me, all upset and hollering 'Stop the

line! Hold it up! Emergency! Error in schedule for Etienne! Stop!'
and so on. It amazed me how much he could say without taking
so much as one breath."

"And?" (Get *on* with it, for Heaven's sake…for *my* sake, actually. I didn't want to have to strangle Etienne.)

"They stopped the line … and here I am." He shrugged.

"I'll have to remember to thank Carstairs the next time I see
him," I muttered, facetiously, under my breath. To Etienne, I said,
"And then what?"

"Well, all sorts of people came around, including one of the
archangels. Archangels rarely get involved unless there's a real slip-
up." He paused. (Etienne must know all of the archangels by now,
I thought. But I remained silent and sat on my hands, just in case
the urge to strangle him became too pronounced.)

"Anyway," he continued, "there really was an error in the
reborning schedule. It seems there are two couples with identical
names in the same town. The couple I'd originally chosen is not
due to have a baby for a few weeks. The other couple, chosen by
someone else, is due to have their baby tomorrow night. We had
some hustle finding Fidor, the rebornee legally scheduled for the
couple, and getting him in place."

In spite of myself, I found my usual curiosity returning. "What
would have happened if you had gone instead of Fidor? Would he
have had to wait and go to the people you were supposed to get in
a few weeks?" I sat beside him on the floor and wondered why I
bothered having a couch.

"Good Heavens, *NO!*" He was aghast. "If I had gone in error,
the poor woman would have had to have a miscarriage, a stillborn
infant, or lose me during my infancy so the record could be set
straight. Fidor would have gone on later, after a decent interval. It
happens often enough, but this time, at least, it was narrowly
avoided and a lot of pain and heartache was spared. I'm very glad
for that family …" He looked into my eyes, "… and, I'm espe-

cially happy for myself, so I can now remain here with ... now ... at this time ... with ... because I ... ah ... I ..." He wound down like a toy whose battery had suddenly lost its spark. He looked at his feet.

He was sort of nice in a quiet and gentle kind of way, like a warm blanket. Neither he nor the blanket was expected to do too much, but both were very comfortable to have around if/when you might need them. WAIT! I caught myself before falling into the reaches of Etienne's eyes, his voice, his ever-improving presence. Wait just a little minute, I warned me. Had I just thought "having around when you needed him" about *Etienne*? Yes, I admit, I had. Luckily, fast on the heels of that aberrant moment, rationality returned and I remembered that blankets had never given me one ounce of difficulty, except once in a while if they fell off of the bed, but, Etienne? Where had he been when I'd needed him all of those so many times during my life? What the hell sort of G.A. was he, anyhow? Inept ... that's what sort.

"Rellie? Are you all right?" he was asking.

"Huh? Oh, yes. Yes, I am. Sorry, I was off somewhere."

"Is something wrong?"

I stood up. "Would you like a cup of tea?"

"Sure, that would be nice." He looked up at me thoughtfully.

"Be back in a minute," I told him, "use the Earth Views screen if you like, I mean, you'll recognize the people, you were ... are ... my G.A."

I went into the kitchen to make the tea. It would have to be regular tea, I'd no arsenic in stock. Waiting for the water to boil, I had to admit I had no idea how we got the things we did. Once a week I filled out a slip of paper with all of the items I wanted, put my name and cloudlette number on it, and placed it in the nearest Request Box, similar to an American mailbox, but in highly attractive pastel shades of pink, blue, and yellow. Within hours, voila! There were my items put neatly away in the appropriate places within my cloudlette domain. Perhaps I could ask for Etienne to disappear?

It didn't take long to get the tea started. I could hear Scott's voice in the other room. Etienne had obviously tuned in on Earth, *my* Earth. I wasn't at all sure how much more I could take in one day. It had been status quo the last Id looked; it should be left alone for a while.

Etienne called in to me. "Rellie? Need any help?"

"No, thanks." It was very nice of him to ask and I felt he would have been happy to help if I'd taken him up on it. Hmmmm....

"Okay. Hey! Scott's off to work."

How thrilling. I put a couple of cream-filled pastries onto a plate, put that on the tray with the tea things, and went into the living room.

Etienne stood up. "Here, Rellie, let me help you with those things." He took hold of the side of the tray nearest himself. Once I was sure he had it, I let go. It *was* rather pleasant to have help. I'm afraid many males had been only too eager to welcome and embrace the Women's Lib thing as an excuse to avoid manners, allowing it to invade and destroy any residual sense of gallantry they may once have possessed. Many males never "got" it. Etienne, for all of his missing things, did appear to have grasped this fact at least. Nice.

We settled down to our tea.

"May I ask you a question?"

"Sure, anything," he answered.

"What has happened to your family? I mean, do you watch them often?" Maybe that's why he'd watched what was happening to me so little of the time.

"Rellie, I've been here so long that most of my family are here or reborn. You are the only one I watched." His eyes bore into mine again.

I'd have to watch that eye contact stuff. He was very good at it. Time to change *that* subject. When I think of all the years and years and years I had longed with an actual physical ache for a man to look at me in the way Etienne was now looking at me.

"I've been wondering something else," I said.

"What?"

"If a person has been here before, how come they don't remember? Have *I* been here before?"

"Yes, you have, Rellie. Several times."

"I haven't been able to get it right yet, huh?" I laughed. "Seriously, why don't I remember?"

"Because it's designed that way. The reborning process takes care of that for you," he explained. "You can request a copy of your complete Existence Record if you want it."

"When I was alive, why didn't I remember having been born before and living on Earth before?"

Etienne sighed the same sort of sigh I had used when my children went through their "Why?" stages. He took a sip of tea, put the cup on the tray, and got more comfortable. Was this going to take a long time?

"Every baby is born remembering everything," he said. "It's the process of living in the day-to-day world that takes care of the forgetting in time. In some people, the forgetting isn't total; in a lot of people, there is that feeling of *deja vu,* of having seen something or someone before. You've had that." It was a statement.

"Yes," I agreed.

"That feeling can be trusted. It usually means you have been in that particular place before, or in a place quite similar, so a memory has been triggered. Your reactions to people you've never met can be interesting as well. You've had occasion to see someone in a crowd, at a train station, in a mall, and for some reason you feel an immediate, strong dislike, or even fear, for that person without even talking with them or knowing them in the slightest, right?"

"Not often, but yes," I admitted. In spite of it all, this was interesting. "Go on," I encouraged him. That was a first, to encourage Etienne in anything except leaving.

"Quite simply, your essential selves, souls if you prefer, have encountered one another previously and with not-too-wonderful results." He picked up his teacup and took a long sip before reaching for a pastry. And then he did it again, caught me totally unaware, unprepared. He looked into my eyes and said, "It explains love, too, Rellie."

Just when I thought he was safe, when I was lulled into a false sense of security, he has to go and ruin it. Just like in that old song '… and then you go and spoil it all by saying something stupid like I love you.'

"How could that be, when Cupid is zinging arrows right and left and up and down so indiscriminately?" My dander was up.

"Cupid is given a lot more credit than he deserves in that field. Love, I mean. He's a figurehead, a marketing success, but a paper tiger in actuality." He tried for my eyes again, but I was on to that trick and turned my head to the left just a smidge while feigning great interest in the section of the floor under my left foot.

"How can you say …" I was interrupted by a loud banging sound from across the street. A new cloudlette was being installed. Saved by a cloudlette! I turned to find Etienne standing behind me. I had nearly run into him. He would probably like that. It came as a shock to realize I was wondering how it would feel to be held against his chest. Good grief.

"Look, you're busy, so I'll go on home for now. You study." He smiled his gorgeous smile.

"'Bye, Etienne." I smiled, not because he was leaving, but because I had enjoyed his visit.

As he walked away, he turned and said, "We'll discuss love again only when you're ready, Rels." With a wave he was gone.

I found myself hoping I hadn't hurt his feelings while, at the same time, realizing my concern was an overt admission that Etienne actually *had* feelings.

It would be best to change the direction of my thoughts and to study.

CHAPTER 8

$\mathcal{I}$ spent the next two days and nights pouring over my books and maps, cramming for my Acceptance test. I wanted to get it done, successfully, the first time. I did stop briefly toward the middle of the second day, when my eyes would no longer focus, to have tea with Thelma.

Etienne stayed away, although he sent one perfect (typical of Heaven) white rose with a card: "Good luck on the exam. Love, Etienne." Only *he* would remember that of all the flowers in existence, I prefer white roses. He'd learned something in all of his guarding years, at least. I put the rose in a crystal bud vase and propped the card next to it, telling myself I was just too lazy to throw it away.

On the morning of the test, I awoke afraid to move. It was like when I had crammed in college and been afraid I'd trip on my way to the exam and dislodge all of the material clinging to the edges of my overburdened brain. I had about three hours to kill until I was to sit in the same auditorium where Thelma and I had heard Saint Peter speak not so long ago. For some reason I don't think I will ever be able to explain, I decided to relax in front of my EVR. I tuned in to Marissa, who was becoming more beautiful by the minute. I caught her as she was leaving on a class trip to historic Philadelphia, Pennsylvania. I thought her teacher had a good idea going to Philadelphia, even though the kids lived in the suburbs only a few miles from the city limits. As is often the case, people tend to visit far places, keeping those near home for "later," perhaps reasoning that those sites will always be accessible. Often those are the places we never quite get around to visiting, unless company from out of town arrives and requests a tour.

By the time I'd made a second cup of tea, Rissa had joined her friends on one of the ugly orange school buses. The noise coming from within the three buses combined into a din, the likes of which can only bring tears to the eyes and memories to the heart.

I settled down to watch, congratulating myself on my wonderful idea to pass the time until the exam. Rissa and her classmates had a beautiful, clear spring day for their trip. The bus drivers were being serenaded. "Here's to the bus driver, the bus driver, the bus driver" their discordant voices echoed inside the orange metal shells of the three buses, "who's with us today." Were the drivers happy about this? Happy or not, I can guarantee they would have been surprised if this didn't happen at least once during a trip. The drivers on the first two busses were smiling that tolerant smile adults get when faced with innocent, exuberant shenanigans. The driver in the third bus, Rissa's bus, was grimacing. He looked as if his hemorrhoids were acting up. Rissa and her friend, Jamie, were discussing their assignment as they bounced along the Schuylkill Expressway toward the Vine Street exit.

"Now," Rissa was saying, "we're supposed to go to five historic sites and then write a paper discussing their significance in Pennsylvania history. Where do you want to go, do you think?" She cocked her head, her long brown pigtail slipped over her shoulder.

I watched with amusement as Jamie extended her hand, upon which she had written a tentative agenda.

After they alighted from the bus, I watched as they agreed on their course of action and made the necessary corrections on Jamie's hand.

I watched as they headed to see the Liberty Bell and were almost run over by a horse-drawn carriage in the middle of Market Street.

I watched as some fleet-footed, slippery-fingered young men bumped and robbed a few tourists in the area to which my granddaughter and her friend were headed.

I noticed a little gray-haired bag lady leaning against a wall of the Public Ledger Building. She tightly clutched the filthy rope handles of a bedraggled paper bag as if she guarded the Crown Jewels.

I watched as Rissa and Jamie laughed with the simple joy of being alive, out of school for the day, and together. They did not notice the fellow staring at them so intently. I did.

I watched as a young fellow sauntered around the corner across from the lady with the bag. I watched as *he* watched Rissa. His eyes scared me. He was, literally, *drooling* as he watched her every move.

I watched and clutched the sofa cushions so tightly a few eider-down feathers drifted in front of my unblinking eyes.

I watched and found myself praying. After all, this should be the perfect spot for that sort of thing.

✳✳✳

I was not the only one who watched Roger, although I was unaware of any of their names at that point. The one I would come to know as Juan stood beneath a tree in Independence Mall, watching as well. When he saw the two girls and appreciated their antics for a few moments, he also noticed Roger lurking at the corner, his eyes somewhat glazed, his body tense as he, too, watched Rissa and Jamie.

"Damn it!" Juan muttered. "He's gonna screw this up *again*. The dude doan know how to keep a low profile. I'm gonna hafta get rid o' him, maybe today. Can't afford shit like that goin' on in the middle of an operation. Later, on his own time, he can do whatever turns him on, but NOT NOW!" He headed toward Roger, his stride purposeful and powerful, his fists clenched as tightly as his jaw.

Meanwhile, Mike was busy with the stolen wallets, extracting not only the cash but also the automatic teller cards and driver's licenses. He was amazed at how many stupid people there were in the world just ripe for the Hellraisers. Mike did his work at an out-of-the-way teller machine, one in the shade and off the beaten path of tourism. It seemed ideally placed at that location, solely for his personal use. He had discovered that many people use their birth date or a combination of it as their personal access number to the machines. All Mike had to do was use the card, fiddle a bit with the date on the driver's license, and out the money would slide into his eager and grubby hands. Gifts just poured out! This was a hell of a lot better than those one-armed bandits down in Atlantic City. Man, you had to put money into those things before any might, just might, maybe come back out at ya. What the hell, on the street, the money was guaran-fuckin'-teed right here at home without any initial expense. By the time the tourists called their banks, the Hellraisers were a lot richer. Mike took back what he considered a "finder's fee." For every hundred dollars he squeezed from a machine, he kept ten for himself. He realized Juan wouldn't appreciate such a thing, but what Juan didn't know wouldn't hurt Mike. How could he find out? It wasn't as if Mike kept the little receipts the machine spit out for you.

While Mike did his job, Otis and Chun moved to the back of Congress Hall into the shade of the park beyond a little cobbled street. Here they continued to ply their nefarious trade, running every so often to deliver the goods to Mike at the machine. Thus far, he had coaxed nine hundred dollars out of the machine. It was time to move on to another well-stocked machine. It could spell a good night, a high night.

✳✳✳

Mister Robert headed toward the corner currently occupied by Emma. He had just left the very park in which Otis and Chun were "working." He did not like that bunch of young hoodlums and preferred to leave as soon as he spotted any of them in the vicinity. He had nothing to steal, which made him feel more vulnerable to the ever-changing dark moods of such persons. He was old for the streets, nearing seventy, and not as able to defend himself as once he could in the old days, days when he worked as a trolley car driver. Those were the days when, after a long day's work, he was met by his wife and two small daughters, and not by the bottles of bourbon that slowly replaced them. After they left him and the trolley car no longer ran, the tracks now long since taken up from the streets, he found himself homeless. It had seemed a sudden occurrence, although he knew it really wasn't. How he managed to live from day to day, he had no idea. He knew his wife had died a few years back, saw it in the newspapers he picked up every day from a park bench. His daughters were married, according to one of the papers, and both were living on the west coast. One of them had a boy, his grandson! When he was sober—which was when he no longer could find a bottle with anything in it—he wondered if he could go out west, find his daughters, and visit with his grandson for a few minutes, just so he could say "howdy" and maybe hug him once, just the one hug to carry with him on the lonely nights. That's all he wanted. He wouldn't get in the way and he'd leave without embarrassing his children as they had so often told him he did. Just one, short visit. He sighed and rubbed his rheumy eyes. The drinks helped him accept it was probably not going to happen, but a man could hold a dream, couldn't he?

He enjoyed the part of the day when he could see the little lady at the corner. She was quiet, but he could tell she liked to see him, too. He made up his mind that he would talk to her this day. He would get her first name, offer his to her: Robert. It was foolish for two old people not talk to each other, if for no other reason than to pass the time. In one way, it seemed he had so much time, but in another, he knew this was not the case. Besides, he was curious. What was it she had inside that danged bag? The fact that she clung to it so fiercely indicated it certainly was valuable, to *her* at any rate.

Time was running out.

CHAPTER 9

$\mathcal{I}$t was with pure joy that I continued to watch Rissa. What a wonderful child! I missed her greatly, but no longer with an aching heart. She was doing well; she was happy and healthy; she was loved. She was fine. Even though I was in Heaven, I had no way of knowing the status quo would change abruptly in a few moments.

I refreshed my tea, stretched my legs, quickly named ten of the archangels in case that was on the test, and watched the screen.

Rissa and Jamie managed not only to look at the Liberty Bell ("Wow, look at that crack. Okay, let's go.") but to cross Chestnut Street without further ado. They zipped in and out of Independence Hall quicker than I thought possible, then proceeded to enter Congress Hall at the corner of Sixth and Chestnut Streets, across from the Public Ledger Building. I noticed the swarthy-looking young man was there and still drooling over Rissa; his terrible-looking eyes never left her. As I watched the two girls enter Congress Hall at the side entrance, another scruffy young man came striding over to the drooly one. The second fellow was obviously very agitated, his fists were clenched, his eyes were ablaze, and his entire Gestalt screamed "angry."

"Roger!" The angry-looking one growled through clenched teeth, as he approached the dribbly one, whose eyes suddenly opened wide. He stopped in his movement toward the door through which Rissa and Jamie had gone, his initial intention to follow quite clear.

"Juan, baby! How's it goin'? I was jus' ..." He took one step toward Sixth Street, his eyes shifting nervously from side to side.

"You was jus' what?" Juan had come within ten feet of his quarry and was gaining fast.

Roger shrugged his shoulders, reached out his arms, his hands palms up in a gesture of supplication, and stepped back two steps. "I was jus' ..."

Juan was upon him. "I'll tell you what you was *jus'!* You was *jus'* goin' to hassle them two girlies, the cute ones that *jus'* went into this here old buildin'." He dismissed the historic and elegant Congress Hall with a wave.

"Juan, no!" Roger cried, his voice rising. "I swear, man!"

"I've told you and told you to leave the pussies alone when we're workin'! You never listen. I doan need a piece of shit like you in the gang. You're fired!" Juan shook his fist in Roger's face. "And, doan go gettin' any fancy ideas about gettin' back at us neither. All I need is to hear one little tiny word, even if it ain't true, and you're dead meat. Got it, ass wipe?"

Roger, for all of his bravado, was not an especially brave person, but all he'd done was *look* at two pretty little girlies. He felt justice had not been served with Juan's cavalier dismissal. Besides, there was usually a vote. They were a democratic gang, after all. This was unprecedented. He could not allow this to happen.

"Jus' like *that?* You can't do this, Juan! I demand a vote of all members. I'm entitled." Turning his back in dismissal, Roger headed across Sixth Street toward the Public Ledger Building at the corner.

Juan followed at his heels, enraged, which was never a good condition in which to put him. "*Entitled*, my ass! Doan ever tell me *can't! I'm* the boss. *I* say what happens and what don't. *I* say you're through, done, finished ... *fired*. That's what you are."

During the "firing" of Roger, Mister had joined Emma at the corner. Instead of their usual silent Changing of the Guard, he sat down beside her on the window ledge in the sunshine. It felt so nice and warm beneath his threadbare slacks. She was stunned and remained seated. She instinctively moved her bag to the sidewalk beside her feet and clutched it against her leg.

Mister smiled. He did not want to frighten her. She was lovely.

Emma smiled. She didn't feel scared. His smile was sweet.

"Hello," Mister said. "I would very much like to talk with you some time when you feel like it. I was hoping it might be today. What do you think? Do you suppose we could talk, just a few words, today? Now?"

Emma was surprised, but pleased. But what did she have to say that anyone would want to hear? She nodded her head just the smallest bit and smiled shyly once more.

He saw the nod, was overjoyed by it. "My name is Robert," he said. "Would you do me the honor of telling me your name?" He made no move toward her, simply sat still, afraid she would run like a frightened deer, if he so much as took a deep breath.

"Emma." It was whispered so softly he could barely hear her.

"Emma. What a wonderful name. Hello, Emma." He offered her his hand.

"Hello, Robert," she gently placed her small hand in his for the briefest of moments before reaching for her bag, loathe to trust it to only one hand, as the crowds thickened at the corner.

"Why, Emma, I wonder if you would like to remain on this corner for the afternoon, so we can talk a bit?"

"Oh!" Her eyes darted nervously as she saw Roger, with Juan behind him, cross the street toward them. "Oh, no. I couldn't. I must get away from here right now!" She stood.

Robert stood; his manners were still in tact after all the years. "Well, perhaps another day, Emma? I would like that very much, and I look forward to seeing you again tomorrow. Have a good day!" He performed a little bow and was surprised at how disappointed he felt as she turned to leave.

During this encounter, Rissa and Jamie toured the second floor of Congress Hall. "Touring" is not really the right word, because it connotes a bit of information gathering, some attention paid to one's whereabouts. This is not how they did it. However, they were gleaning just enough knowledge to prattle about it, should the teacher require it, as they had learned teachers are prone to do after school trips.

They looked into the Senate Secretary's office, the Conference Room, and both the East and West Middle Committee Rooms before poking their heads into the Senate room, which encompassed the rear of the second floor. It was here, for a reason Rissa would never discover, that Jamie stopped dead still and said: "Oh, Rissa! I'll meet you outside, just give me a minute, would you?"

Rissa readily agreed, although admitted to a great amount of confusion. No one was close; the room was empty of people. There was a fireplace on the east wall. All that stood were wooden desks in two semi-circles in obeisance before one chair in the center of the room. What did Jamie see in that room? (If anyone had cared to ask, a very good-looking, and young, janitor had passed through the room and she was hoping he would return. He didn't and she felt a need to seek him out, leaving Rissa "in extremis.")

Rissa shook her head, sending the pigtail swinging across her back, and went to sit on the wood settee in the hallway on the landing between the "up" and "down" staircases to wait for her friend. She scuffed her sneakers back and forth on the random-width wood floor. Jamie seemed to be taking an inordinate amount of time down the hall. Rissa decided to wait for her out front, where there were lots of people, things happening, and fresh air to breathe. She took the "down" stairway on the west side of the building. From the landing between floors, she could see the street corners on both sides of Sixth Street at Chestnut. She saw what appeared to be two young guys arguing, one of them obviously afraid of the other who was following him across the street, apparently yelling the entire way. He turned his head for a quick moment and Rissa recognized the good-looking fellow Jamie had seen near the Liberty Bell. What was going on?

As she stood waiting for Jamie, she was very interested in the two guys. She watched them head for the far sidewalk where two grungy street people were having a conversation. She briefly wondered what they could have to talk about, when the two people stood up. The man had a brown bag under his arm, probably booze she thought, and the woman was mangling a paper shopping bag as she clutched its handles tightly in her fists.

What occurred next happened so fast that Rissa would initially be accused of not knowing exactly what she saw. This was not true, because she had had ample time to observe the participants previous to the "incident."

✳✳✳

I saw it coming and could do nothing about it. I clutched my cushions tighter, tighter than even Emma could have grasped her precious bag. Why it had to be my Rissa in that spot at that time, I quickly put out of my head, because of my own experience of being at the fabric softener at the wrong time. But this was different; this was my *granddaughter!* I could only sit there, tensing in every part of me that could tense, my forthcoming exam totally forgotten.

I watched.

CHAPTER 10

At the moment Rissa was about to continue down the stairs to wait outside for Jamie, she saw Juan catch up to Roger. The one guy looked so very angry and the other so very scared that Rissa remained at the window to watch what might transpire, her hands resting on the railing in front of the window. Someone had opened the top portion of the window a few inches, presumably to provide some fresh spring air to the mix inside.

"You sonofabitch bastard!" Juan shouted over and over again, his angry voice drifted upward to where Rissa stood, quietly watching the scene below the window. He reached out to grab Roger by his shirtfront as Roger leaped to his left, swinging his left leg into Mister Robert's hip and causing him to loose his balance, a not too-steady thing at the best of times. Emma's eyes widened at the sight of her friend in trouble, but she was wise and backed up, planning to leave as unobtrusively as possible and head for the park. Primed and ready for flight, she did watch as Roger again kicked Mister Robert, who had managed to struggle to his feet and start to brush his threadbare jacket sleeve of the debris picked up during its encounter with the sidewalk. This second kick sent Mister sprawling onto his nose, which began to bleed profusely.

Emma no longer thought; she reacted. Her friend was hurt and she had to help him. He had been nothing but polite and kind to her. She took a tentative step toward the two brawling, screaming young men who were now yelling obscenities while shoving and punching each other all over her precious corner. No one offered to help Mr. Robert; it appeared to be up to her to help her friend. Standing with her feet flat on the sidewalk and her shoulders straight, Emma made one enormous effort and swung her precious bag at Roger's head, the Bad One who'd kicked Mister Robert. The blow, while paltry, was the last straw for Roger. He seized Emma's prized bag and tossed it into the heavy mid-day traffic on Sixth Street. With one giant shove, he sent Emma flying after her bag. Mister Robert was once more on his feet and tried feebly to reach for Emma. He was too late. As concerned as if Emma had been an annoying gnat, Roger resumed his battle with Juan.

Rissa (and I) were transfixed as the traffic on Sixth Street continued south according to a green light, unprepared for Emma being catapulted into the road directly into the path of a red Honda. Rissa's screams went unheard by those outside who were, by now, paying attention to the event and screaming as well.

Mister Robert took charge with alacrity and did a fine job. He told someone to call 9-1-1 as he fearlessly strode into the traffic, held Emma's head in his arms, and spoke softly to her. She was bleeding a great deal, but he could not ascertain from where it was all flowing. She was not conscious, but she was breathing faintly.

"Excuse me, ma'am," Mister Robert called to the lady at the food concession cart parked near the corner, "would you be so kind as to hand me that bag over there by the curb?"

The woman did so, holding it with the tips of her fingers, obviously loathe to touch it. Emma's bag was much more dirty than previously and had sprouted a new small tear on its side, but it was saved. But could *she* be saved?

The very shaken driver of the Honda had stopped immediately, pulled over to the curb, and gotten out. He was a young man in a lightweight gray summer suit. He was thoroughly unnerved at the events that had befallen him and the injured woman in the street. His pallor matched his suit and he looked as if he would like to cry. "I didn't see her, I swear I didn't! She just shot out into the street from nowhere!" he kept repeating.

Others who had witnessed the fellow running into Emma, but missed the events leading up to it, tried to comfort him. "You couldn't have known she would fly into the street like that; it's not your fault." But the young man could only shake his head and run his fingers repeatedly through his soft brown hair. "I didn't see her! Oh, my lord! Is she dead?"

Emma wasn't moving, but the consensus of opinion was that she was alive, although seriously injured.

Matters managed to become even worse and I could do nothing but continue to watch them unfold. Rissa was no longer frozen in place, but rushing down the stairs two at a time, pushing open the heavy front door of Congress Hall, and running to the corner. It was obvious she wanted to help Emma in some way. As she reached the fire hydrant with its red paint chipped at the top, revealing it had once been blue, Juan and Roger ran back across the street toward the hydrant where their argument had begun. Their fight was suspended.

"Let's get the hell outta here!" Roger shouted to Juan.

"I'm not finished with you yet, dick!" Juan growled as they both slammed into Rissa, who jumped away as if burned.

In that instant, both young men and Rissa recognized each other. Juan was slippery, a man at home with quick changes in situations. He recovered first by snatching Rissa's purse, a tiny black leather one on a long strap that looked big enough for a dollar bill and a lipstick, little else. Dangling from her arm, where it had slipped during her dash for the corner, it was easy to relieve her of it.

"Doan say nothin', babycakes, or you're next! You seen nothin' and it better keep that way if you wanna go on breathin' 'cause I know who you are and where to find you! I've got your I.D. now."

The boys had made the assumption that Rissa had been standing there by the fireplug all along, witness to the entire episode. It didn't matter that she had seen everything from the window above where they stood, because the result was the same: she had seen. Juan was correct and, therefore, Rissa was terrified. Juan waved her purse in the air before both fellows instinctively bolted for their place along the Delaware River. They were out of sight long before the ambulance came to take Emma to the emergency room at nearby Pennsylvania Hospital, the nation's first hospital, founded by Benjamin Franklin and Dr. Thomas Bond in 1751.

Mister Robert walked the several blocks to be near her, to get news of her, his still-bloody nose forgotten. He heard himself praying, something he'd not done in many years. He carried her bag tightly by the rope handles, his own forgotten on the corner sidewalk where, if he had looked, a brown puddle spread beneath it.

"Rissa, where are you?" Jamie asked as she turned the corner to see her friend slumped against the western wall of Congress Hall, shaking.

CHAPTER 11

I bounded up and immediately started to pace. My exam was forgotten. That thug had my granddaughter's address! He knew what school she attended. Her driver's license and school identification card were in that silly purselet, and now that criminal had them. Damn! What would he *do* with them? I was more frightened than I remember being in a long, long time.

I went to find a friend, anyone, someone. Thelma was not at home. I had to find Etienne! I admitted to needing him at this time in my life, er, existence. I'd take no test this day. Instead, I would go out and purposely look for Etienne. Heretofore, that would have been a totally alien concept to me, but Hamlet spoke no truer words when he said: 'There are more things in Heaven and Earth, Horatio, than are dreamt of in your philosophy' (*Hamlet*, Act I, end of Scene V).

I left my cloudlette without turning off the EVR where Rissa was stammering out her story to the amazement of Jamie. The ambulance siren squealed as it bore that poor lady off to emergency. Two mounted police had arrived upon the scene, their horses standing stock still as people gestured, yelled, and pointed to Rissa. I heard the concessionaire lady say, as she too indicated Rissa across the street, "I think she saw the whole thing and so did some dirty street man who hangs around here every day." The woman was correct, but her presumption, too, that Rissa had watched from where she now stood was in error.

I ran up and down the Heavenly streets dearly wishing I had paid closer attention to the road maps I'd been given. Because I had no idea where Etienne might hang out, my activity could only be described as random, frantically random. Persons in Heaven do not ordinarily run. There is rarely a need to hurry around here, so my frenetic movements were noticed by a great number of people. This was to my advantage, because I not only ran, but called to each and all who looked my way: "Have you seen Etienne?" To which I received as many answers as people I questioned. This added considerably to my frantic behavior.

When I found myself visiting the same places repeatedly, I calmed and started thinking instead of simply reacting as a crazed mother hen. "Okay, okay, Debarelle," I said to me, "*Think!*" I was winded and plunked myself down onto a little roadside cloud puff to catch both my breath and my mind, breath being the easier to find.

I greatly regretted telling Etienne to leave me alone. To be honest, I never believed he would listen to me, his record of hearing whatever I had to venture as far as an opinion or a request was extremely poor until now. *This* time he listens. What was I going to do?

"Hi, Rellie!" said a most cheerful voice in front of me. He had bent over to speak to me.

"ETIENNE!" I jumped up so fast I clunked him in the chin with my head. I grabbed him by the arm. "I am *so* happy to see you. I've been out looking for you all over Heaven! Where in Heaven's name have you *been?*"

"So I heard from just about everyone. Calm down, Rellie, and tell me all about it," he said, taking my arm with one hand and rubbing his chin with the other. We sat on puffs next to each other. He smiled his gorgeous smile and remarked, "I'm touched that you feel a need for my presence, I really am."

"Don't let it go to your head, it's advice I'm after and Thelma wasn't at home, some closed-door meeting her note said." Even in my current state of upset, I remembered to avoid eye contact with this man.

To give him credit, he did not comment on the fact of his being my second choice, but entreated, "So, here we are … tell me all about whatever it is, so I can bestow my best advice upon it." He smiled once more.

I told him everything from the moment I'd awaken ready for the test through my decision to relax with the Earth Views Receiver prior to heading over for that test. I admitted how stupid my decision now appeared and that I was no longer in any shape to take a test.

When I finished, Etienne was quiet for a few moments as if collecting his thoughts (here, again, I was assuming he had some to collect). "First of all," he said more firmly than I'd ever heard him speak, "you *will* take that test. Furthermore, you *will* pass it on your first attempt. It's not for another hour so there's plenty of time for you to calm down and get over there. I'll walk with …"

"NO! I can't possibly do it! I've forgotten everything and couldn't begin to think right now. Hell, I can barely breathe. It's out of the question, Etienne, so don't even talk about it. And you don't need to walk me anywhere as if you don't trust where I'll go!"

"Rellie, if you want me to help you, and I *can*, you will listen to me for a change. You must take that test; furthermore, you must pass that test. Only by doing so can you qualify for sitting in on an Intervention, if it becomes necessary for us to help Rissa." He gently forced my chin up with one finger and made eye contact with me.

Drat!

"Intervention?" Hope began a soft hum in my heart. "I don't remember reading about that in my handbook. Are you making this up?"

"No, you know better than that. I may be a bit of a stumble bum once in a while …"

"That's an understatement, if ever one was uttered."

"… but you know full well that I am, beyond a shred of doubt, honest. I would never lie to you, Rellie."

I did know that and said so.

"Intervention is not mentioned in your handbook, because it is strictly the province of guardian angels. It is presented in great detail in the special *Guardian Angel Study Guide* each of us receives as a trainee. There are two types: Simple Intervention and Complex Intervention. I've personally seen the complex variety used only fifty times in the entire time I've been here. It was, to reassure you, successful each and every time. That's a one hundred percent success rate …"

"I know my math. Get on with it, this isn't a board meeting." I was not being very nice, but what the hell. (Oops.)

Exasperation was apparent in his voice, but he continued as if I'd not just been so rude. "*If* you take the test today. And *if* you pass it, *then* you'll be in a position whereby you can request, then witness and/or advise on an Intervention of either type, though it sounds right now as if a Complex might be needed. That way you can feel you are doing something to help, while keeping an eye on Rissa's activities. There may be no need for it, but you should be prepared."

I had to admit, grudgingly of course, what Etienne said actually made sense. I was surprised. I might have to further evaluate this man. What a mess. It was, by far, so very easy to just be upset with him. "His heart's in the right place." Thelma's words echoed in my spinning head. She might be correct after all. Damn! (Oops.)

"Okay, Etienne, what you say makes sense," I admitted out loud. He smiled sweetly. "BUT, why isn't this Complex Intervention thing used more often? Is it dangerous? All it sounds like is a little bit of a shove and assistance from Above."

"I've never used it myself. Never saw a reason to," he said. He raised his hand and added, before I could retort, "You were never in a situation that qualified for it, so save me the sputter." Ouch and touché! He had a spine after all. Hmmm.

"I do *not* sputter!" I sputtered.

"Yes, well … anyway. Don't get me wrong, you were a regular customer for Simple Intervention. Gadzooks, yes. I was kept spinning many a time doing those. It got so I was extremely proficient at 'em." He sat tall, exhibiting a bit of a cock o' the walk attitude.

"You're showing off," I said.

He continued as if I'd not spoken, shifting a bit on his little cloud seat. "It got so I am looked upon as one of the authorities on Simple Intervention, others often ask my advice on it."

"Good grief, Etienne! What the hell *is* it?" He was the most exasperating being I'd ever known or ever wanted to know. Times were tough here and all he could do was blow his own horn. He didn't get to do that much, I suppose, but still …

Etienne stood, brushed some nonexistent cloud lint from his left sleeve, and put his hand out to help me up. I brushed it aside and stood, glaring at him as I did so.

"I was only being polite, Rellie. Let's start walking over to your exam while I explain Intervention, Simple and Complex varieties," he said, extracting a little dog-eared book from his pocket. I caught sight of the title, *The Guardian Angel Guide*, before he opened it to a well-worn section.

"I'll read a short synopsis of Complex Intervention to you first." He dramatically cleared his throat, put the book in front of his nose, and began: "Complex Intervention in Heavenly procedure is diplomatic and vigorous hands-on interference by one guardian angel within the territory of another with that guardian angel's express consent and joint participation. It is considered inappropriate under customary Heavenly procedure to thus intervene without first bringing the intention to the Complex Intervention Committee for vote. Intervening guardian angels usually state that they are intervening to protect their own guarded person and to defend themselves against possible demotion in the event the Intervention should fail. Participating guardian angels must give their consent; however, it is the petitioning guardian angel who is solely responsible for the Intervention's success, both to the committee and, ultimately, to the Heavenly Council. Complex Intervention is acceptable *only* when done for humanitarian reasons or under the 'collective Intervention' terms of the Heavenly Charter to preserve peace and security in an Earthly territory, no matter what size."

"Wow!" I'd stopped walking.

"Yes, it entails a lot of pre-planning and legal work; it can involve a lot of folks. Cooperation and careful timing are paramount to its success," he once more cleared his throat for effect and flipped back several pages. "Simple Intervention," he read, "is just what it sounds like: simple. It is immediate and direct interference in the life of your guarded person." He looked at me. "Do you remember the time when you were about fifteen years old and went fishing with your boyfriend, that goofy kid with the ten-mile high cowlick in the center of his head?"

"Sure, but he wasn't so goofy. He was kinda nice." We started walking again.

"He was definitely goofy, believe me. He grew into a goofier adult, tried making spandex bracelets and earrings for a living. Died when a bungee cord broke. Goofy."

It takes one to know one. "So?"

"You two were so busy goo-goo-eyeing each other that you didn't realize, until quite late in the day, that your anchor had lost its grip on the bay's sandy bottom and you had drifted out into the ocean, with no land in sight and a storm raising up!"

"Oh, *that* fishing trip. Yes, it was something. A lovely dolphin swam up beside the boat as the water was coming in faster than we could bail it. I pet the dolphin and it stayed with us until a large cabin cruiser tossed us a towline and got us safely into the bay. Such a sweet dolphin."

"I sent her."

"What?"

"I sent her *and* the cabin cruiser, one to comfort you and one to actually help you. *That*, my dear, was a Simple Intervention. But, let me tell you, arranging it was not the simplest of tasks, why, I had to first find the closest dolphin in the area, convince her to alter her afternoon plans, and then ..."

"Thank you, Etienne. I appreciate it." Then I did something I could not explain; I stood on tippy-toe and kissed his cheek, still seriously avoiding his eyes.

He blushed. Good grief, but he blushed a rosy pink. His hand went to his freshly kissed cheek. From the look on his face you'd have thought I'd given him a million dollars. Because no one here in Heaven gives a dwaddle-diddle about money, I guess that kiss was worth a lot more to him. As soon as I was back flat on my feet, I regretted my impulse. I realized too late that it wouldn't do to lead the dratted fellow on, he was buzzing already. Well, it was done. I'd have to make sure not to repeat that impulsive gesture, but when someone tells you how they saved your life, it's easy to get demonstrably appreciative.

"That's just a little example of things we G.A.s are able to accomplish for our charges on Earth, Rellie." I wasn't quick enough and he gazed into my eyes as if all the stars in the firmament were there, then he continued to tell me, "I want this information to comfort you and also to give you incentive to pass the test today. We are always better off prepared in a possible crisis."

"Thank you for saying 'possible,' and thank you for your help. I will give it my best in there this afternoon."

We had arrived at the test site with fifteen minutes to spare. The steps were swarming with N.A.s like me, all nervously waiting to take the exam.

"If you like, I'll wait here for you," Etienne said.

He'd been so nice that the quip I wanted to utter just would not pass my lips: 'Leave me alone, I'll be fine.' Instead, I nodded, joined my compatriots, and entered the building. Let me pass this test; let me be able to help Rissa, if she needs an Intervention of any type. Now was not the time to think about any of that. I had a test to pass.

CHAPTER 12

According to the clock high on the wall, he had been sitting in the emergency room waiting area for forty-five minutes. Sitting? More like up and down, sit a while, pace a while. Robert found it interesting to realize how much of his life was spent sitting. But this sitting was different; there was no semblance of relaxation; it was filled with great worry about his friend. "Emma," he whispered softly, liking the sound of her name upon his lips. "I have your bag and will take extra fine care of it. Please get well so we can have our chat."

The emergency room was busy, but not as hectic as it would become by evening. Something about the night seemed to create more patients. Even now, doctors, nurses, and technicians rushed about like ants in a maze to minister to the sick and injured. Somewhere behind the automatic double doors lay Emma. She was gravely hurt, that much Robert realized.

Robert waited as he sat in a plastic chair that provided an unrestricted view of the doors through which Emma had been taken. Occasionally, he wiped his bloody nose with the damp paper towel he had taken from the men's restroom where he'd gone to wash his face, to become more presentable. His nose was sore and the bleeding had slowed considerably. He didn't care about that annoyance; he just wanted Emma well. Twenty minutes ago, he had politely asked the receptionist if he might know how she was, if he might go in to hold her hand and be with her for just a little while.

"What's the patient's last name?" he'd been asked.

"Why, she's a new friend and all I know is her first name … Emma," he'd told the woman.

"You're not a relative, then?"

Robert thought that a rather silly question following the information he'd just provided. "No, ma'am," he'd replied sadly.

"You will have to wait over there," the woman indicated the waiting room with a weary wave of her hand. "As soon as we know something, we'll let you know." She was busy but not unkind. Robert had to be satisfied with that for the time being. He had been waiting ever since, but his worry grew along with the minutes.

***

While Robert waited and worried, Rissa quickly recovered. After filling Jamie in on the entire event, she had to repeat it to the three police officers who had arrived on the scene. The young driver of the red Honda was taken to the police station a few blocks away, as were several other drivers who could attest to the suddenness of Emma's appearance in the road, although none could say for sure how she'd gotten there. A search for Rissa's teacher ensued. She was found sitting in the pleasant park behind Congress Hall eating a famous Philadelphia soft pretzel smothered with the almost-obligatory bright golden mustard. This was the same park through which Juan and Roger had retreated from the crime scene at full speed. The teacher accompanied Rissa to the police station, after sending a loudly protesting Jamie off with several other girls who had exited Independence Hall. Rissa had to repeat her story once again. There, she would await the arrival of her parents, who had been notified of the incident, and not return to school on the bus with the rest of her class.

***

My examination was lengthy and all-inclusive. It took four hours to complete. When I was finished, it was sent through a scanner and graded immediately. I passed, not with flying colors, but my score wasn't anything to be ashamed of either. When I saw "Passed" stamped on the front of the exam booklet in a bright phosphorescent red, that was all I cared to know.

True to his word, Etienne was waiting for me when I left the building. One look at my face and he knew I'd been successful. His face lit up with a grand smile as he shook my hand. He matched my rapid pace as I headed to my cloudlette, my EVR, and news of Rissa. "Marvelous! Congratulations! Good job! I'm proud of you! This is gr …"

"Thanks. What's happening with Rissa? Have you checked?"

"Yes, I checked my hand-held EVR, and she's in the happy custody of her loving parents. All in all, she's had rather a fine time of it. She identified a few of the mug shots …"

I groaned. My granddaughter, that sweet child, mixed up with mug shots. Incredible.

"… and all efforts are being made to locate the boys. I'm afraid her purse is a different kettle of fish, though. In my learned opinion, it's toast."

"*Boys*! How can slime like that be referred in human terms?"

"It's hard to fathom, isn't it? Anyway," Etienne said, "we'll check it all out when you get home. Don't forget the party tonight."

He elaborated upon the party. I found it hard to imagine myself attending an Acceptance graduation party when my heart and mind were so full of worry, but it would be in bad taste not to show up for a little while. I accepted his invitation to escort me, but agreed to stay for just an hour. He had the sense not to argue with me. We were definitely making progress.

✳✳✳

Juan and Roger scrambled under the bridge, panting for breath, their fight forgotten in their harried dash to their hideout. Mike and Chun were already there, half asleep from the beer they'd been drinking since eleven o'clock that morning. The beer was a self-rewarded perk for their work of the day. No one had seen Otis since the last run a few hours previously. Some of the other gang members sauntered in, most with shiny, glassy, red-rimmed eyes. "Yo" was the accepted form of greeting.

Breathing in short gasps, Juan ignored the others and roughly shoved a surprised Roger into the gravel at their feet and said, "Youse better hang onto youse balls, mister, if that little girl identifies you. We can't afford to have the cops come crawlin' around here, so I want you to get lost, go over to the Hotshots for a while."

"Effin'-a, I don't have to do that! Shit, man, it's cool. That chick's nose was so far up her ass, no way she's gonna finger me. Wait an' see; it'll be cool. No sweat," Roger tried not to sweat as he attempted, unsuccessfully, to pull back from Juan. He did not remind Juan that he had "fired" him earlier.

Grabbing his left ear in a tight grip, Juan turned Roger around until their noses were touching. "I dint *ask* your opinion. I *told* you to get your ugly ass on over to the Hotshots for a while. If I want you to come back, I'll let you know. Notice I said 'if,' not 'when,' asshole." He shook Roger before letting him drop to the ground in a heap. "Got it?"

Roger rubbed his ear, which hurt like hell. He did not like the Hotshots. The leader was Juan's baby brother, Paolo. Damn it, the kid was only thirteen, the *oldest* in the stupid gang. Hell, it was more like a juvenile delinquent club than a real gang. Juan was demoting him over there? No way, Jose! They'd just see about that. But he knew he had to play it smart for the time being.

"Sure, man, whatever you think's best. I'm outta here." He left under the glaring eyes of Juan, but he was not going to the Hotshots, no way. Juan wasn't gonna boss *him* around any more, no little kiddie groups, no siree. "Son of a bitch," he mumbled under his breath. "Wait an' see, Juan-baby. You'll be singin' a new tune through a new mouth. Soon."

CHAPTER 13

Emma was drifting ever so nicely on air as soft and warm as down feathers. She had the sensation of lying down without any armrests poking her. It was the nicest feeling, but another sensation was making itself known—pain. What hurt, she could not quite make out, but it felt as if every bone in her body could use a bit of comfort.

She wanted very much to open her eyes, to see the pretty trees in the park above her head, to watch the clouds float past and hear the birds sing, but she was extremely sleepy. Perhaps later she would open her eyes. Yes, she would rest for a bit. First, however, she must check on her bag, make sure it was safe.

A nurse on her way past the cubicle in which Emma lay with i.v. tubing inserted into her arms, saw Emma move her right hand as if patting the bed beside her. She watched as the hand moved more vigorously, covering more of the bed area as if searching for something and not finding it. Then the woman seemed to panic. "Agh, agh …," the nurse heard her call around the tube in her throat. "Help, help," Emma was sure she was crying. Both of her hands moved now, threatening to remove the i.vs. Emma became increasingly agitated when she realized that she could not locate her bag.

As the nurse attempted to calm Emma, her eyes fluttered open. When she realized she was not in Washington Square Park, her panic became wild, her eyes opened as wide as saucers, and she yanked and tugged at every tube entering her body. Gone was the lovely drifting feeling; the pain was temporarily gone as well. Memories rushed at her. Mister Robert was hurt! The Bad Ones had done it and she'd hit one of them with her bag. Her bag. On, no! Did they have her bag? Where was Mister Robert? Her ring? There'd been a red blur in front of her and then she was hurt, in the street. A car must have hit her, maybe a bus she felt so bad. Now she was here with these people dressed in white. Was this Heaven? Was she dead? No, not Heaven, because of the pain. There should be no pain in Heaven. Must be a hospital. Where was her bag? She could rest if only she had her bag. Hands kept holding her, but she had to fight them, had to get up and find her bag.

"What's gotten into *her?*" one nurse asked the other.

"I don't know, the poor thing must've taken quite a blow to the head; she's wild."

"Maybe I should get that old man out there waiting for her, he keeps asking about her. Maybe he could help calm her down. She's going to hurt herself more and she's got so many internal injuries already," suggested the first nurse.

"Go ahead, I'll try to hold her, but hurry back with him," replied the second as an intern came over to assist. He had a syringe in his hand.

Emma continued to struggle but weakened quickly, pausing long enough for the needle to be inserted into the i.v. in her right arm.

"There," said the intern, "that should take affect soon and calm her. What a tough old bird!" He walked away to assist elsewhere. The nurse remained by the side of the bed, making soothing sounds close to Emma's ear and patting her gently on the arm.

Who's that buzzing in my face? Emma wondered. Is that who took my bag come back to torment me? I want to cry. I'm so tired. After I sleep, I'll go get my bag.

The nurse pulled the curtain aside and led Mister Robert into the cubicle where Emma lay, still somewhat agitated and mumbling unintelligibly as her head moved from side to side.

"Sir, you can sit in this chair beside her," the first nurse said. "She's had a tranquilizer and should be more relaxed soon. If there's any problem, push this button; we'll be at the nurses' station across the hall," she said as she handed Mister Robert the long cord with the call button at the end. Both nurses left him alone with Emma.

Tears came to Mister Robert's eyes as he looked at his friend. She was a small woman, but now she looked ready to blow away. Large, ugly bruises were beginning to show on her arms and face. Blood had dried at the corner of her mouth; cuts and scrapes appeared up and down her arms, some of which had been sutured. Her legs were beneath the sheet, so he could only imagine the condition they might be in. She looked so vulnerable lying there, and for the first time in his recent memory, he felt a deep need to protect someone, to keep this little lady from further harm. She had braved a punk kid to try to help him. Imagine anyone thinking he was worth defending, when he hadn't felt much like defending himself! But this woman hadn't hesitated in doing so.

Gently, and with some reverence, Mister Robert put his hand on Emma's, careful of the tubes that were comforting and nourishing her body. "Emma," he whispered ever so softly. "Emma, it's me, Robert, your friend from the corner. I've come to see you."

At first he thought she hadn't heard him; she had become so very still. As he watched, afraid to blink, she struggled and managed to open her eyes to look full into his face.

He smiled at her.

She stared at him.

"Emma, you are in the hospital near the park. You were hurt by a car and brought here to get well. I've got your bag." He held it up for her to see.

She battled her pain and favored him with one of the nicest smiles he ever remembered seeing. "Thn y.." she said groggily around the tube in her mouth.

"You are most welcome. It is my great pleasure to help you. Is there anything you need me to do for you? Name it and it's yours," he said.

"Yzzz…"

He leaned closer to better hear her.

"Rnggg … give rnggg …"

"Did you say 'ring,' my dear? If so, where is it?"

"Bggg …"

"Ah, this marvelous ring is in your bag, is it? That is an easy request, one to which I shall respond immediately. Lie and rest while I find it." He placed the bag on the bed where she could watch as he opened it. Instantly, he saw the string hanging down on the inside, pulled it up as one might a bucket from a well, and found the little gold band tied at the end. "Here it is, and lovely as you are, my dear." He held it close for her to see.

Emma's mouth turned up at one corner, the largest smile she could muster. It was okay!

"Would you like to wear it, Emma?"

Caaa'n…"

"Ah, can't, is it? Won't it fit?" He gently tried the ring on each of her fingers. No, it wouldn't fit the gnarled fingers. What to do? "I'll tell you what let's do, I will tie the ring around your neck, how would that be? I've two shoelaces my shoes don't really need. They should do the trick quite nicely, don't you think? What do you say?" He was amazed at how very good it felt to be doing something for someone, to be needed. When was the last time that had happened? No matter, it was happening now.

"Yzzz," Emma agreed to the plan. She was feeling dozy.

After sliding the ring onto the joined shoelaces, Mister Robert carefully and with great ceremony, tied the ring around his friend's neck, making several tight knots for good measure. "Yes indeed, that looks just right, Emma, just right." The little ring lay in the center of her chest, the overhead lighting caused it to sparkle in the dismal little cubicle.

"Thn … y …" And, with that, her energy was spent and Emma slept, her world a better place because of Mister Robert, such a kind man, such a good friend. If only he could make the pain go away.

"You'll have to go now, sir," said the doctor as he entered the cubicle. "She has to go for a CAT scan and some other tests."

"Will she be all right?" Mister Robert stood reluctantly.

"I can't answer that right now. Please, it will be some time. Go home, relax, then give us a call later."

Go home.

"Yessir." Mister Robert glanced once more at Emma, pat her hand softly, and said, "I'll be back, my dear. You rest and get well." With that, he left to go back to the streets, to go "home" as he'd been advised.

CHAPTER 14

everal days passed uneventfully, both in Heaven and on Earth. Rissa, none the worse for her experience, was back in the swing of things at school and with her friends. Emma was critical with massive internal injuries, but continued to hang on, although the prognosis was not good. Mister Robert was allowed to visit with her and he did so every day without fail. Much of these visits was spent sitting by her side, patting her hand, and whispering to her. Rarely, now, did she open her eyes. Whenever he left her side, Mister Robert went directly to the little church around the corner, a change in his prior behavior of begging outside taverns. Lately, he didn't seem to have the time to go to the taverns.

Roger, meanwhile, lurked about by himself. He had once sneaked back to the hideout while Juan was away and only little Tony and his idiot buddy, Leland, were there sleeping something off. He knew all of Juan's stash spots, so it hadn't taken long to find Rissa's little purse. He removed her driver's license and school identification card, leaving the purse where he'd found it. He stole a bicycle from an open garage on Elfreth's Alley, rode to the western suburbs, and began to stalk Rissa.

For the first two or three days, Rissa had no inkling of Roger's activity, until one afternoon as she and Jamie sat on the stone wall at the back of the school building to watch the lacrosse team practice. Jamie was in "love" with just about every player.

It was a lovely day, not too hot, but with bright sunshine and a clear blue sky. The leaves on the trees were abundant and lusciously green as a result of the heavy rains of the past few months. The girls were enjoying the sunshine, talking as they turned their faces toward the sun to start a tan they'd enhance over the coming summer months by the pool.

Roger leaned the bicycle against a tree at the opposite side of the field from where he could watch the girls closely. Yes, that was both of them, the ones he'd seen at Independence Mall the day the road toad got hit. He felt no responsibility in Emma's accident; as far as he was concerned, she was no more human than the stolen bike on which he now rode. She'd been in the way; he'd gotten her out of the way. Why anybody'd be so upset about one less piece of scum floating around the streets lookin' like shit, he had no idea. His mind did not allow the concept that gangs and their members could be *personae non grata;* in his warped mind, gangs were a *culture.*

As he observed the girls, he was particularly interested in Marissa, as her license called her. She was as pretty as any girl he'd ever seen or touched, but this one could spell big trouble for him if she identified him. He knew she had gone to the pig barracks, that was standard procedure, but he did not know, for sure, if she was able to pick him from the mug shots. The picture in the book was almost two years old. Hell! He'd matured a lot since then. He was an adult now, for shit's sake. Back then he'd just been a little kid.

Roger's criminal history was extensive for one only sixteen years of age. When he was eleven, he went through a period of placing false alarms to fire and police departments. At twelve he borrowed his older brother's .38 special and took it to school tucked inside his coat sleeve. He made the mistake of showing it off in the boys' room at lunchtime. Some goody-two-shoes caught the little circle of admirers surrounding him and the gun and reported him. Not only had he gotten in deep trouble about that, but was suspended after beating the crapola out of the stooge. Later, to make matters worse, he had to explain to his brother why his gun was in police custody, which was not an easy task considering that Wayne was never sober and never slow to throw a punch. Wayne got into deep shit with the authorities. Roger lost three teeth for that episode and learned to sleep with one eye open. Now Wayne was twenty and in jail for armed robbery, but Roger continued to sleep with one eye open. The year Roger was fourteen he was busted a couple of times for possession of marijuana. He lucked out each time, because he was never caught with enough to make a charge stick, each time he'd just sold most of his load. He had to laugh at his luck. But two months after his fifteenth birthday, he was caught touching girls. It seemed to him that the girls liked it, but they ran home crying to daddy afterward. He had a strong fondness for young girls, ones whose little titties were just tiny nubs pushing themselves out into the world; ones whose tender butts were firm as cantaloupes under their tight jeans; ones whose eyes were innocent one minute and frightened the next. It was superb to be a master of manipulation and control. One day, Roger knew, he'd want to do more than just look and touch, but he had to find the right girl for that. The sluts that hung around the gangs, the groupies, they were too easy, too eager and willing. No, he wanted a virgin, a pure little girl who'd have tears in her eyes, a little filly he could tame and control, one who'd fear him and respect him. One totally unlike his whore of a mother who let anything with a dick come at her. What a bitch! She'd ignored Wayne and him, no wonder Wayne was in prison. She never went to see him. Either she was too drunk or too busy with her latest boyfriend of the hour. His old man? Not even his mother was sure who that was. The dude he had called his father had lived in the house until Roger was six. One night, after Roger went to bed, he heard his mother being beaten and rushed out to help.

"Daddy, daddy! Don't hit my Mommy!" he had cried. He got a split lip for that bit of misdirected heroics. His father had caught his mother sucking off some dude out in the back shed. She got a broken arm for her endeavors. His "father" left her lying on the floor at Roger's feet and was never seen again. Roger quit school the day after his sixteenth birthday, seven months ago.

The sound of giggles drifted across the field and brought Roger back to the moment. Rissa and Jamie were walking across the field toward him, waving to some of their friends on the bleachers near where he sat. He didn't move, but kept his eyes on them. He wanted them to see him. He had something to say to the pretty broad, Marissa.

***

"Let's turn that off for now," Etienne said, reaching for the knob on my EVR.

"*Now?* Touch that and you'll sing soprano in the Heavenly Choir, I promise." I grabbed his arm, ready to dismember him if necessary. "Turning that off now would be like running the movie, *Heidi*, on television near the end of the fourth quarter of a football game. The only difference would be *I'm* the only one who'd want to maim you, not an entire nation of sports fans. I could be worse."

"Okay, okay, I get it!" Etienne pulled his arm away and sat back down on the rug. He chuckled. "I remember that game. Well, nothing's going on right now and you'll get upset and picture all sorts of eventualities, like you've always done. What a worrier I had to contend with; it was not easy."

"Being my guardian angel had to have been a breeze, you hardly *did* anything, *I* did all the work. What'd you do, but let me suffer. It was mighty difficult being your guardee, let me tell you. If I'm ever a G.A., I sure as hell will work at it; I'll take it seriously. I hope Rissa's G.A. is a responsible one who knows his right from his left."

"She."

"Okay, she. Does she know her left and right, up and down? Are there more male or female G.A.s in this place?" I asked.

"Hell? This place? Rellie, I know you're upset, but be careful," Etienne scolded. He was so proper. "To answer your many questions, you will soon be receiving a detailed synopsis of my activities in your behalf over the course of your Earthly existence. You will have the opportunity to review it, to ask questions and demand explanations, if you so desire. You, Rellie, will then grade my performance in your behalf. This grade will go to the G.A. School headmaster and be placed in my permanent file, along with other reports from my previous G.A. performances."

He looked most serious, not one smile wrinkle around those eyes, eyes I now dared to look into—briefly. "Etienne, this is taken very seriously, isn't it? I mean, I know how important guardian angels are to each person, but I never realized the extent to which Heaven goes to maintain professional standards."

He smiled at me as a parent would to a difficult child.

"So," I continued, "could you get demoted if I hand in a bad report? If I prove you goofed too many times? If I complain too much?" Did I have that much power over this not-quite-so-total fool?

"You would have to prove beyond a shadow of doubt that I had failed you both in practice and in my heart. I know I did not; I wish you knew it, too." He sounded so very sad.

I was surprised at my reaction, but I said, "Well, time will tell, won't it? I won't jump to any more conclusions until I see that report. Frankly, I can hardly wait to see what you did other than send a dolphin and a boat. I suspect you wore yourself out on that one day and had to rest for the entire remainder of my life."

"At present there are ten percent more male G.A.s than female, but statistics change weekly. Rissa's G.A. is Penelope. It's her first time in that capacity."

"Oh, great. A novice." I groaned.

"No! Think about it, Rellie. She's gung ho about the assignment. She's an over-achiever, just like Rissa. She was graduated third in her G.A. class of 150,000 and immediately signed on with Rissa, before your daughter gave birth to her. Not to worry about Pen, she's terrific!"

Giving no quarter, I mumbled, "Well, we'll see about that. I sure hope so."

"She knows left, right, up, down, sideways, in, out, and every direction of the compass, all the stars' names … she's marvelous." He sighed.

I heard something in his voice. "Etienne! You're in love with her, aren't you?"

"Yes, I love her," he answered quietly.

My reaction surprised me. I leaped up. "You miserable excuse for a…a…You're no better than men on Earth! You're a hypocrite, a jerk. Ever since I arrived here, all you've been able to say is that you love me, blink those puppy-dog eyes, and send over white roses. What's going on here?"

During my tirade, Etienne had risen to his feet. He now put his hands onto my shoulders and forced me to drown in his velvety eyes. Somewhere, deep inside, a part of me was turning to mush. "I'd no idea it mattered so much to you. I've been scorned so often by you, I was devastated. Now you sound as if you care. It would sound almost as if, dare I hope, you are *jealous*!" He spun around the room, his arms outstretched. "YES! YES! She *does* love me!"

"Get a grip, Et." Jealous? *Me*? Because of *Penelope*?

"Pen's my little sister." He grinned.

"Oh, shit."

CHAPTER 15

Five days after the accident, Mister Robert arrived at the hospital eager, as usual, to see Emma. He had taken some still-pretty cut flowers from a Dumpster behind the florist shop a few blocks from the hospital. They would surely help Emma feel better. He'd present them and, if she still didn't have the strength to open her eyes, he would ever so carefully pat her hand on them so she would know what they were.

As he walked down the hall, he realized his step was almost jaunty. What time he and Emma had wasted in politeness, shyness. Well, that was over. Now they would have each other. Good heavens, between the two of them they might be able to actually *do* something for themselves. He hadn't felt such hope in a very, very long time. Nearing the door to Emma's ward, he straightened his shoulders and held the flowers high. As he entered the room, he instantly knew something was very wrong. Emma's bed was empty. The other occupants of the room, those who were not asleep, would not look him in the eye.

"Gone." One elderly lady whispered from the bed at the end of the row near the window.

Mister Robert hurried down the center aisle to her side. "Please, ma'am. Have they taken her for more tests? Where is Emma?" He was beginning to feel frightened.

"Gone. Wheeled out late last night. Woke me up."

NO! His mind screamed. She must have been moved to another room. She can't be ... NO! His legs wouldn't support him; he sank onto the cold metal chair beside the woman's bed, the flowers forgotten as they fell to the worn gray linoleum flooring at his feet.

The old lady had drifted off to sleep.

Twenty minutes later the ward nurse, Molly Lander, found Mister Robert in the chair, his eyes staring vacantly into the room.

"Sir? Are you all right?" She put her hand gently on his shoulder. He seemed such a nice man and so devoted to poor Emma.

Blinking in surprise, Mister Robert looked up at Molly. "Wh..? Oh, yes, I'm ... Where's Emma? Has she gone for more tests? Will she be back soon? Should I wait for her here or come back in a little while?" He picked the flowers from the floor, held them out to Molly. "I brought these to cheer her up, to help her get well." He smiled a tremulous smile.

There was nothing for it but to tell him the truth, thought Molly. It was hard, but it had to be done. Kneeling in front of him, she placed a hand on the one without the flowers. "Sir, I am so sorry. Emma passed away early this morning, just after midnight." At the sight of his stricken face, she said once again, "I'm so sorry, sir. Is there anything I can do for you?"

Shaking his head, he got up and walked over to the bed where Emma had slept, where she had died alone. With great reverence, he laid the little bouquet on the empty bed. "These are for you, Emma," he whispered in a voice so full of love, the nurse began to cry as she left him alone for a few moments. The other patients were now, mercifully, all asleep. When Molly returned, the man was gone; the wilted flowers still lay on the uncovered bed in silent, lonely testimony of friendship and respect.

✳✳✳

"Murder, now it's *murder!*" bellowed Sergeant Ramsey, who was in charge of the case he referred to as 'Scumball 1,000.' "Find Roger Kravin," he yelled to those within hearing, "and find him *now*. It's second-degree murder for that young punk. The old lady died early this morning. FIND HIM! I want his balls in here pronto."

There followed a briefing. The search was on. The word was to bring in any of the Hellraisers a cop could find. Roger Kravin was out there, and now was the time to locate him, before he ran, before he realized the woman had died. There wasn't much time, word traveled fast on the street. The sergeant was also troubled about what might happen to the young girl who'd identified Kravin. Those creeps had her purse, her *i.d.* God alone knew what they'd do with that when they heard the old lady had died. Timing was critical.

***

"Don't look now, Rissa …"

"Where?" Rissa turned completely around.

"I think it's that guy, the one from Independence Mall, the one you said pushed that bag lady into the street …"

"Omigod! Where, Jamie?" Rissa grabbed her friend's arm as they stopped walking. "*Where?*"

"Act normal, for Pete's sake, will you? And start walking!" Jamie ordered.

They continued across the field at a much slower pace, Rissa still clutching Jamie's arm. "WHERE IS HE, JAMIE!" She insisted, squeezing Jamie's arm for emphasis.

"Ouch! Stop that! I bruise easy." Jamie wrenched her arm from Rissa's grasp. "He's sitting over near the end of the bleachers, on the first row by the water fountain." She had enough sense not to point. She rubbed her arm.

Rissa wasn't listening to anything but the rapid beating of her heart. It was *him*, the one who'd pushed that old lady into the traffic, the one who'd hurt the man, the one who was buddies with the jerk who stole her purse. It was the one she'd identified at the police station. He had to be pretty bad to have a mug shot on file already; he didn't look any older than she was.

"It's him, Jamie. Why's he *here*? He's from the city, for Heaven's sake. Do you think he's following me?"

"Oh, Rissa, that would be horrible!"

They weren't left wondering for long. As they approached the bleachers at the center of the field, Roger sauntered down toward them.

"Hello, ladies. Isn't it a fine day?" He lifted an imaginary hat.

Both girls ignored him and tried to move away toward their friends in the upper seats. Roger followed.

"Marissa, stay here. You," he said, roughly, to Jamie, "go away like a nice little bitch and sit with your snooty friends."

"N-no, I'll stay with her." Jamie defensively crossed her arms in front of her chest, but didn't budge.

"No sweat, maybe you should hear what I've got to say to this broad after all, so's you can make her see reason." His smile showed no pleasantness.

"I don't want to hear anything you have to say. Go away or we'll call the police." Rissa said, as she turned to climb the bleachers and get away from him.

"Hear this and hear it good. Keep your damn mouth shut, bitch, or you'll be sorry you was ever born. You saw *nuthin'*. Make sure it stays that way, or trouble will be your best pal. I'll know what you're doin' every step of the way, so doan get no fancy ideas from your daddy or the cops. I know where you live, which bedroom is yours … nice ruffles on them blue curtains. Sleep tight, sweetheart." And Roger walked away. They watched as he mounted a bicycle and rode away.

"Oh, God." Rissa sank onto the hard wooden seat closest to her. "Oh, Jamie." She was too shocked to react; she simply sat there, her eyes were open but not focused on anything. "Oh, Jamie! What can I do? Did you hear him? He talked about my *bedroom*. He followed me to school. He's *stalking* me. I've seen enough of those real-life crime shows to know that. Know what?"

"What?" asked Jamie, now seated beside Rissa.

"A lot of the time nothing can be done about it until the person being stalked is hurt," Rissa said, "or killed," she added in a small voice.

"No. That's just not going to happen here," Jamie tried to reassure her friend. "If you just keep quiet like he said and wait for that old lady to get better, then you all can go back to normal."

"Are you kidding? I identified that jerk to the police. Even if the woman gets well—and, I sure hope she does—he's still in big trouble. The police aren't going to forget it and let it go back to whatever *normal* is. That idiot will blame me no matter what. No, I've got to tell the police about this right now." She stood. "And you'll come as a witness. Let's go, I've got to find Daddy and he'll go with us." Once again she took Jamie's arm.

Grumpily, Jamie mumbled, "Okay, just let go of my arm. It has not been a good day for this arm." She held the sore arm close to her side.

The girls hurried back across the field to the parking lot behind the school. Rissa had borrowed her brother, Alex's, car for the week while he was away at some brain camp. Tucked under the wiper blade on the driver's side was a folded piece of paper. Rissa was tired of car wash advertisements showing up in this fashion and grabbed the paper, ready to toss it into the garbage, but she noticed it was handwritten. After settling behind the steering wheel, she unlocked the passenger door so Jamie could get into the car.

"Here's a note from somebody, let's see what it is. I could use some good news right about now," she said, as she unfolded the paper. "No!" She exclaimed and dropped the paper as if it were on fire.

Jamie retrieved it from among the gum wrappers on the well-worn black car mat at her feet and read: "Shut up if yu no whats gudd for yu." She looked at her friend.

Rissa turned the key in the ignition and gunned the gas pedal. "I don't like this, I just don't like this. Keep that thing and let's get over to my father's office at the bank."

***

"*Nothing's* going on right now?" I couldn't keep my voice down.

"Well, er, it wasn't. I sometimes forget how quickly things can happen down there," Etienne offered by way of expiation.

"Right. Now what can we do? Let's get that complex Intervention thing started." I leaped to my feet and headed toward the doorway. Etienne remained rooted to the spot. "Are you coming with me?"

"Where?"

"To file the necessary papers, get things rolling …"

"You have to talk to Pen first, bring her up to date. I've no doubt she'll cooperate fully, but Rissa is *her* charge, not yours. Pen is the one who needs to initiate the proceedings."

It's such a hard pill to swallow when he's right. It's doubly worse, when he's so calm. Once again, he was right. This was happening much too often lately for my comfort. He was definitely smarter than he looked. I went back and sat beside him on the floor to discuss the order of events.

As we sat immersed in this trouble, Thelma arrived, grinning from ear to ear. I had *never* seen her look so happy and she is a very happy person. She was outdoing even herself this time.

"What?" I asked. "Come, sit." I pat the carpet beside me.

"No, I couldn't possibly sit, not for one little millisecond!" she grinned so widely I thought her mouth would bleed at the corners.

"What? Something's obviously happened to make you so happy. Thelma, that smile on your face would make the Cheshire Cat look like he was grimacing. What?"

"Ian's on his way! He should be here by tomorrow!" She did a quick little spin around in the center of the floor. "*Tomorrow!*"

She squealed with joy and broke into the song from the Broadway show, *Annie*. "The sun'll come out tomorrow..." she sang in a clear alto voice.

"Ian?" I realized two things simultaneously that surprised me no small bit. First, I hadn't thought about Ian in days. Secondly, I was happy for Thelma, not wondering where I fit into the event. "That's wonderful, Thelm!" I stood.

"You really and truly are happy for me, aren't you, Rellie?" She always knew how I felt before I did.

"I really and truly am," I said. "It surprises the hell out of me, but I really and truly am." I hugged her.

"Oops! You must wipe that word from your vocabulary; it's not wise around here. The New Arrivals Committee chairperson just told me Ian will have a cloudlette beside mine. Isn't that divine? Must run, but I wanted to share the news. You'll come with me to the main gate tomorrow to greet him, won't you, Rellie? I know he'll want to see you."

"No, I've got some stuff to do. After he gets settled in and you've caught up on things, give me a call and I'll pop over." My mind was again engrossed with the Rissa business; after all, Ian would be here for a while; there was time for all of that later. First things first.

"Okay, see you later." Thelma smiled her way out the door. "Tomorrow, tomorrow, I love you tomorrow; you're only a day awaaaaaaay..."

"Wow!" Etienne came over to my side. "Are you all right with this?"

"Yes, believe it or not, I am. Thanks for asking."

"I lo ... I care, Rellie."

"I know."

CHAPTER 16

I tuned my EVR to Rissa as she breezed past her father's secretary and swept into his office, Jamie in tow.

"What are you doing here, girls? While this is always a pleasure, to what do I owe this lovely intrusion?" Alex was seated behind his desk, papers neatly piled before him, a file folder open on his lap. He raised one eyebrow at his daughter.

"There's a problem, Dad," Rissa didn't soften him up, knowing from experience that he was bottom-line oriented. He liked to back up from the punch line.

"Ah, and it couldn't wait for another hour until I got home?" He pushed his chair backward, closed the file folder, and placed it on top of one of the piles on his desk. He was now totally tuned to his daughter. Maybe it had to do with an increase in her allowance. Her mother did not like to hear such discussions and preferred him to deal with them.

"Well ..." The telephone at the corner of Alex's desk chose to ring. Mary, his secretary, let only those calls through she knew for certain he would want to handle directly. She was a treasure. Reaching for the phone, he said to the girls with a wink, "Excuse me, I'll get rid of them unless it's your mother ... hello?" He leaned back into his chair.

"WHAT?" He sat up quickly, white-knuckling the receiver, his eyes wide and staring at Rissa. "Good lord, that's terrible! Yes,

yes. I'll be sure to tell her, as a matter of fact, she's sitting right here, just came in to see me. Yes, yes. Tomorrow for sure. Thank you for letting us know. Yes, you too."

He hung up the phone and turned to the girls. "That was Sergeant Ramsey downtown. The little bag lady died early this morning."

"Oh, that's awful! She was just trying to help her friend," Rissa exclaimed. Jamie nodded.

"Yes, she was and now she's dead. Do you know what that means?" Alex asked, but continued without waiting for a response. "It means that boy, that Roger person, is now wanted for murder and your testimony is even more valuable to the police. I told the sergeant we would come down tomorrow and talk with him about it after I call Bill."

"Do I need a lawyer, Dad?" Bill Watson was her parents' attorney.

"You…*we*… most certainly need his advice. We have to decide if you should testify."

"I have to, Dad! I saw the whole thing and that lady is dead. I want to do it. I *have* to do it."

"Rissa, those boys know your name and where you live, because they have your purse. They might try something if they are frightened enough, if they think you're a danger to them." Alex did not like these thoughts, but one had to deal with reality.

"Oh," Rissa said in a tiny voice. "That's why we're here, actually. The boy who shoved the old lady into the street came to school today, he …"

"WHAT???" Alex jumped from his chair, knocking pens and pencils onto the floor at his feet. "Are you sure it was the same kid?" He moved close to his daughter as if to protect her from danger.

"Y-yeah, it was him, sir," Jamie said.

"It was definitely him, Dad."

"Oh, my God!" Alex returned to his desk and dialed the phone. "Sergeant Ramsey, please. Yes, this is most certainly an emergency, just tell him Alex Butler is on the phone." While he waited, he said, "Honey, it'll be all right, don't worry. Yes, Sergeant." He relayed what he knew. "Sure, she's right here. He wants to hear it from you, sweetie. Yes, here she is …" And then Rissa told the story so both her father and Sergeant Ramsey could each hear it at the same time.

"Roger didn't know Emma had died when he was at your school today, Rissa. Once he finds out, he'll realize how important your testimony is and how it will work strongly against him and his cronies. It is my fervent wish to apprehend him some time this evening at the Hellraisers' hideout, but I want you to promise me you will be extremely careful, stay home tonight, and stay inside. Let me talk with your father now, Rissa. Be careful. I'll keep in touch. Don't worry."

After his discussion with Sergeant Ramsey, Alex left his office for the day, got his car from the office parking garage, and closely followed Rissa as she dropped Jamie at her house before going home to await her mother's arrival. The family remained home that evening; the doors and windows were locked and double-checked every ten minutes.

I watched all of this on my EVR and wondered what Rissa's G.A., Penelope, could possibly have been thinking when she allowed Rissa to get involved in this mess in the first place. There seemed to be a strong family resemblance between Etienne and his sister, that was for sure; both were bunglers. The world must be desperate for guardian angels if they accepted such material as those two. To think that my family were the beneficiaries of both; it was a thought to curdle one's mind.

✳✳✳

"The word is she's dead, man," Mike told Juan, when he returned to the hideout.

"Who's dead? Your latest chick o.d.?"

"Naw, man. The old broad Roger pushed inta the street. She's dead."

"Who told you that?" Juan demanded.

"Johnny over on Spruce Street. He's been sticking his salami into this deeeelish piece that works in the laundry room of Pennsylvania Hospital, where they took that woman after …"

"I know 'after' already. So what'd this Johnny say?" Juan flicked his switchblade open and started to clean his fingernails.

Mike knew from experience that Juan was his most dangerous when he looked calm and relaxed. He backed up. "Johnny said his whore, who works the night shift, said the word was the bag lady died. Nobody claimed her body, so they bagged her. Funny, right, Juan? Baggin' a bag lady? Get it?" Mike laughed nervously.

Juan swatted Mike in the head. "Stupid shit! Go on, I ain't got all day for this crap."

"Yeah, right, Juan. Johnny asked what happens to a body no one wants and the broad told him it goes to one o' the city hospitals, so students can cut 'em up to practice on before they do it to real people for lots o' money. That's all I found out. Want me to find Roger, tell him?"

"As much as I hate the shit, yeah, find him and bring him back here. They get him, he blabs, we're all in deep shit. Yeah, Mikie, find the bastard. We need to take out a little insurance, so I gotta 'talk' to our pal Rog." He waved the knife at Mike and turned away.

✳✳✳

As he peddled the bicycle along City Avenue toward the city, Roger had no idea anyone was looking for him. He was feeling good, as he usually did after what he considered a good day's work. He smiled and thought, "That chick's face, man! She probably had to go right home and change her little silk undies after I talked to her. I'm gonna do that again." He chuckled, a rasping sound.

As he passed the Channel Six News television station and a little bar across the street, he thought about going in for Happy Hour freebies like he sometimes did in joints downtown, but he wasn't dressed for the part. Money. He'd need to get some more and decided to return to Independence Mall the next day for a few quick grabs. He'd get high tonight and avoid Juan and the rest of the Hellraisers. Maybe he'd get laid. The night was young. Hell, he was better on his own, didn't have to share any booty, boobie, or drugs. He turned right at the Presidential Apartments and headed for East River Drive. Traffic was heavy and he was forced to ride on all the ruts and potholes at the edge of the road. "My balls'll fall off after much more of this crap. All my little children are gonna be dead." He pedaled faster, wanting to reach the wide sidewalk along the Schuylkill River, where it was smoother.

***

As Roger rode the bicycle in traffic, the search for him had intensified. All available mobile units had his description and a flyer had been issued with his photo and vital statistics. An emergency briefing had included data on Roger for all officers, mobile and on foot. Those officers in the historic area around Independence Mall were as alert as always and looking for any Hellraiser gang member they could find to bring in for questioning as to the whereabouts of one Roger Kravin.

***

After he left the hospital, Mister Robert had no idea what to do or where to go. Nothing held any interest for him. He aimlessly wandered the streets, never noticing how blue the sky was that morning nor hearing the beauty in the birds' songs. It seemed an affront to him that life continued as before for the rest of the world. Because it was there, Mister Robert sank onto a bench in Washington Square Park, in front of the memorial wall. He read the large words near the top: "FREEDOM IS A LIGHT FOR

WHICH MANY MEN HAVE DIED IN DARKNESS." Oh, God! Did Emma die in darkness? If only he had been with her, he might have been able to help her; he could have at least called the nurse or a doctor. No one else in that room would have known if Emma were in trouble. Heck, no one in that ward would have realized if she'd suddenly stood on her head and sung the "Star Spangled Banner" in Gaelic, they were all so numb. He put his head in his hands and rested his elbows on his knees. And he cried.

As the minutes passed, so did his tears. He wiped his eyes and nose on a wrinkled napkin that he found in his pocket and noticed some more of the words further down on the memorial wall in smaller letters: "In unmarked graves within this square lie thousands of unknown soldiers ..." A new wave of sorrow swept over him as he wondered what would happen to Emma now. Would she, like the unknown soldiers, lie in an unmarked grave? But she was known! *He* knew her. Following quickly upon such thoughts, Mister Robert realized something would have to be done with Emma's body. But, what? Could some family be found? He didn't even know her last name. *She* had not bothered to remember it. He decided he must hurry back to the hospital and find out. Even though his mission was a grim one, Mister Robert suddenly felt a tiny bit better. Maybe there was still something he could do for his friend after all. Maybe there was a way he could show his love for her ... some how. If only he had some money, he would buy her the prettiest dress and most beautiful headstone it could furnish. And he would visit each day to make sure no trash or cans or bottles were nearby; and he would talk with her, let her know how things were going. She'd been a fine person; he felt certain she was now in Heaven. He hoped she could see him and know for sure how much he cared about her. He prayed for her and that could never hurt.

After some difficulty and much perseverance, Mister Robert was given the same basic information as Mike had received via

Johnny. When a person enters a hospital through the emergency room, Social Services tries as best they can to identify that person and find next of kin. If the person is not identified, and subsequently passes away, the body goes through a Gift Registry process and is ultimately taken to a teaching hospital to be used for research. On the other hand, and this did not apply to Emma, if a person arrives DOA (dead on arrival), the body goes to the morgue. If not identified and/or claimed, the body is cremated at the taxpayers' expense.

"Where is Emma now, this minute?" asked Mister Robert.

"She is at the funeral home where she will wait until Gift Registry has assigned her to a hospital," he was told.

"Which funeral home would that be, please?"

"We are not allowed to give out that information, sir, unless you are family. If you are family, you must fill out some forms and then can claim the body."

Robert thought quickly. "Could you call the funeral home for me? I had loaned Emma a gold ring to wear for luck, even though I should not have done so; it is my daughter's ring. She forgot it during her last visit and I was planning to mail it back to her the very day Emma was hurt. I was so sure Emma would recover, you see, and dear Nora would never have known the difference. She lives in California, you see." He stopped, surprised at his tenaciousness. If he could get the ring before Emma went to a school, then he could bury the ring in a special place. He knew Emma would approve.

The nurse was looking at him curiously. "Well, ah … let me check with my supervisor. Would you mind waiting a minute?"

"I'll wait. Thank you. I'll just sit over there by the door."

"I'll be right back," she told him and hurried to find the supervisor.

After what seemed hours, but was really only twenty minutes, the nurse returned. He stood as she approached. "Sir, my supervisor called the funeral home and they found the ring you described on a some shoelaces around the lady's neck. Apparently, it was too small for her fingers. Does your daughter have tiny fingers?"

"Oh, yes, she does. Very tiny." (Not even close. Even as a little girl, Nora's hands had resembled rubber gloves swollen with water.)

"Well, sir, They're not far from here and are sending the ring over with a delivery person. She should be here in a few minutes. If you'll sign this form while you wait?"

Later, the ring safely tucked inside his jacket pocket and the laces returned to his shoes, Mister Robert felt much better. In fact, he felt so much better, he continued past the park to his afternoon corner at Sixth and Chestnut Streets. Silently, he performed the Changing of the Guard ritual in Emma's honor, before sitting on the window ledge of the Public Ledger Building and looking around. Things were much the same as they had been that day Emma was so senselessly hurt while trying to help him. "Oh, Emma, I should have been able to help *you*."

It was then he made up his mind to find the little hooligan who had killed his friend. Leopards don't change their spots, and eventually the kid would return to the scene of his crime. When he did, Mister Robert would be there. Then we'd see about a little justice. But first, it might be prudent to have a little drink to pass the drearies of the day. He shuffled off to a nearby liquor store. He'd found enough change on the sidewalks and parking lots in the area to afford a pint of bourbon. Yes, that would be nice.

CHAPTER 17

I watched my EVR until Rissa and her family were locked up and tucked in for the night. Then I turned to one of the general news channels for the city of Philadelphia and picked up on the police activity concerning Roger. Dear little Emma had died. Wait a minute! She *died.* For a smart person, I was behaving in a dim manner. It might be prudent for me to hie myself over to the Main Gate Reception area to see when Emma was due to arrive. I doubted a woman who died in an attempt to save another human being would go elsewhere, however, I knew I should check it out.

Etienne had left in search of his sister, Pen. I grabbed my Heavenly map book and set off for the reception area at the main gate. It was a pleasant walk on normal days with people milling about laughing, a gentle fresh breeze blowing off the many lakes and ponds in the area. Today, however, I was understandably preoccupied. Not only was I so absorbed in my worries, but the little birthmark on my elbow had begun to itch as it always did when I was upset. Some things never change. I'd been teased so often about the thing because I had the misfortune to have a birthmark shaped like a mushroom, a mushroom about the size of a quarter. Some of the more risqué of my friends saw a penis, not a mushroom. I can't claim to have ever encountered one (not a mushroom) of that shape, however.

A few blocks from the reception area, I noticed a group of G.A.s assembled at the side of the pathway ahead of me. One of them appeared to be as angry as ever I'd seen anyone in Heaven. The others seemed to be attempting, vainly at that point, to calm him down.

When I drew abreast of the group, I slowed down. I admit to being curious. "I quit! I said it and I've done it!" The angry one was jumping up and down. "Quit. Q-U-I-T. Quit!"

"Seymour! That's fine," said a lovely female G.A. with shiny brown eyes and long silky brown hair curled perkily at the tips. "Our concern is if you did it legally or are you merely ranting?"

"Pen! (*the* Pen?) You know me better than to ask such a thing. Of course I did it legally, by committee and everything. It's been approved just an hour past. You know the rules and, believe me, *this* is one incorrigible bloke. There's no helping Roger Kravin, none. As such, he does not deserve to have a guardian angel; he has lost all privileges inherent in my work. I gave him all the best chances, helped him far more than he deserved. Not once did he appreciate it, just took it as his due. And now, *murder!* Well, I've washed my hands of the fool. He's on his own now for the remainder of his time on Earth … which won't be long, if he continues at his current pace." Seymour demonstrated his feelings by pretending to wash his hands.

"Oh, hi, excuse my outburst," he said when he saw me standing stock-still in the middle of the path.

"Hi, I'm Debarelle. I'm considering entering G.A. school soon (I *am?*) and didn't realize a person could quit. It makes sense, though. What will you do now?"

"Teach, while I await a new assignment. It's a good thing I get no demerits from this case."

I really wasn't concentrating well. It suddenly hit me. "I couldn't help over-hearing. Did you say '*Roger Kravin*'?"

"Yes, that's the case."

"Could I talk with you about it later? You see, I'm off to find Emma, the lady who died. My granddaughter, Rissa, is the girl who witnessed the entire thing, the one being stalked. I'd really love to talk to you about this. Could you come over to my place, say, in an hour? I'm over on Ethereal Way, on the eastern shore of Great Celestial Pond."

"I'd be happy to come over. We'll see what we can do. You know about Interventions, I gather?"

"Yes. I feel this may be the precise situation for one," I said.

"I agree. I must sign a few more forms about my resignation, then I'll meet you at your place." He smiled and waved as he trotted off to his forms, visibly calmer.

I turned to face the pretty girl standing beside me. "Are you, by any chance, Etienne's sister?" I asked her. She informed me, with significant pride, that indeed he is her brother.

Before I could tell her he was looking for her, Etienne ran up to us. "Hi, Rels. Pen, I have to talk to you. Now! 'Scuse us, Rellie. I'll see you later and bring you up to date." He and Pen walked away from the group.

I said my good-byes and headed to the reception area, arriving a few minutes later to find a very large, boisterous, and happy crowd. There were lots of smiles, hugs, and kisses in progress. It was wonderful. Single-mindedly, my eyes searched for one wizened little face: Emma's. My mind was whirling, but for the first time since this awful situation began, I felt more hopeful. Seymour, Etienne, and Pen would help Rissa; they *had* to!

To further illustrate how preoccupied I was, I literally walked smack dab into Ian before noticing him. I'd totally forgotten he was scheduled to arrive today. Thelma stood beside him, her face lit up brighter than the largest star in the skies. Ian didn't look too unhappy himself.

"Rellie!"

"Ian!"

We moved into each other's arms. It felt so natural and so very nice. One of his big old bear hugs was just what I needed at that moment.

"You look great, Rellie! Turn around," Ian directed.

I spun around, pirouetting like a ballerina, a smile on my face.

"Yep, just as beautiful as ever." He grinned, his dear face filled with smile wrinkles as deep as ocean canyons.

"You look terrific, yourself. Welcome to Heaven."

Thelma had patiently waited for us to greet one another, but joined in at this point. "He does look wonderful, doesn't he? Considering all he's just been through." She gazed into his eyes, he into hers. I felt like I'd stumbled into their bedroom by mistake.

"Let's go for tea," suggested Thelma. "It'll take some time for them to get Ian's cloudlette ready. He's going to live right next-door to me, but I think I already told you that." I nodded. "Can you believe the luck? I'd requested it the moment I arrived so many years ago, but had no real hope of it happening. I should know better, considering where we are."

That's when it struck me. I wasn't jealous. I realized when Ian hugged me that I felt safe and content, so very glad to see my friend. But, and it's a big BUT: I had felt nothing sexual or possessive, not at all. What a relief it was, to tell you The Truth. It was stupendous to see Ian again, to know his warmth and wit were nearby. It was also stupendous to see my friend, Thelma, so marvelously happy.

"You guys go for tea, I'll join you later, if I can," I said. "I've got to meet someone and better go find her."

"Is one of your family arriving today? I'd no idea, you never mentioned it," Thelma said. "Bring her along when you join us, won't you?" Her arm was comfortably around Ian's waist, his draped familiarly around her shoulders.

"No, it's that street person, Emma. She died and should be arriving, that is, if she's scheduled for Heaven."

"That's right! Oh, she must be, Rellie. Well, good luck and we'll see you later!"

Echoing her sentiments, Ian turned, "Rellie, please be sure to stop by, we have so much to talk about: Agatha, your demise, everything."

The happy pair walked away toward to the Reception Garden, a picturesque outdoor café at the southern edge of the area.

The Main Reception area was very congested. As I searched for Emma, I was constantly jostled and bumped. Folks reuniting are a joy to behold; you can't help but get immersed in such happiness. I was calming from earlier in the day. It was as if my head were on a swivel. Anyone looking would think I was watching a ping-pong match the way my head bobbed from side to side. Every now and then, I rose up on tip-toe to peer over tall heads.

I had walked around and through the reception area three times without finding Emma. Perhaps she was not coming? What could that sweet little lady have done to fail Heaven? I decided to join Thelma and Ian at the café and turned to walk in that direction. As I did so, the large crystal bell at the Main Gate rang in a second batch of new arrivals. According to my handbook, this was not an everyday occurrence. It was customary to bring in new arrivals once each day. Only when the daily count is extremely high is a second group permitted to enter on the same day, such as during wartime or natural disasters on Earth. It makes sense, because there is a lot of paperwork and organization involved for the arrivals. I've noticed that Heaven likes to keep things as calm and smooth as possible. Arrivals at all times of the day would create havoc. Havoc is not a desired condition in Heaven. I hadn't been fond of it on Earth either.

There she was, entering the gates and looking bewildered. I headed toward her only to be gently nudged aside by a little man with a big smile on his face. "Emma!" That one name was filled with so much love, I could have cried. "Jimmy!" she cried and fell into his arms. "Oh, Jimmy, my Jimmy!"

"Emma. I have missed you so much. It's so good to see you. There, there. You have no more worries and you'll be as warm as you want to be, never cold or hungry or scared again. You're in Heaven, sweet." He held her arm.

"Are you sure, Jimmy? All everyone could talk about on the way was a terrible earthquake in California. I didn't understand." She looked deeply into Jimmy's clear blue eyes. "Are you sure?" she repeated.

"Aye, as sure as my love for you, Emma. You died in that hospital after the rotter pushed you into traffic."

"Yes, yes, I remember. I remember everything now. Oh, Jimmy. After you died in that mine collapse, I lost my mind. I really did, you know." He nodded his head in agreement. "I found myself in *Philadelphia*. Oh, Jimmy!" she said in a small, frightened voice, "I even forgot *you*."

"Sweetheart, you never forgot me, your mind was protecting you from great hurt, that's all. I watched. You kept our wedding ring close to you at all times, remember?"

"The ring! Yes. I knew it was the most special ring in the world. I just couldn't remember why. I wonder what happened to it? Was I buried with it?"

Jimmy escorted his wife over to the café as they spoke. He found two chairs at a small table and they sat. After ordering two ambrosia coffees, he explained all that had happened since her accident. He told her about Mister Robert and his activities in her behalf, he even mentioned the flowers. "He has the ring. He knows it was important to you and is trying to decide the best way to honor you. He is tending toward burying it in Washington Square Park some evening, near the memorial wall."

"That would be lovely, don't you think so, Jimmy?" She sipped her coffee.

"Indeed, it would, Emma. Indeed it would. Nice man, Robert. He does drink a bit much, although I can't hold it too much against the chap. I always enjoyed a bit o' the brew myself." He chuckled.

I was loathe to interrupt their reunion, but I needed to talk with this woman. As I entered the maze of tables on the sidewalk, I could see Thelma and Ian toward the back, heads bent together, deep in discussion. Now and then one of them would throw their head back and laugh with abandon.

Walking up to Emma, I said, "Excuse me?"

She glanced up at me and smiled. "Hello, do I know you?"

"No, not really. My name is Debarelle, but please call me Rellie. My granddaughter, Marissa, witnessed your accident, the one that resulted in you being here now."

"Oh, yes. I'm so sorry. Is she all right? Jimmy, get the lady a chair." He did so, pulling it up to the table beside Emma.

I sat. "Thank you. Yes and no, Emma. Physically, she is fine at the moment, although that, too, could change. Emotionally, well … The kid who shoved you into the street, his name is Roger. He found out that Rissa saw it all happen and has been stalking her, threatening her if she were to carry through with her intention of testifying against him. He's a bad one, Emma."

"The Bad Ones. Yes, that's what I used to call the gang that hung around the Mall area, stealing from those lovely tourists who dropped so much good food into the trash cans."

Jimmy had been listening carefully. "Hello, Rellie, I'm Jimmy O'Donald, the proud husband of this fine woman." I shook his outstretched hand. "I am, also, a guardian angel of the first order and happy to be of assistance, if assistance is what you need." He was a dear little fellow, and I expected he might even salute. He didn't, but he did smile broadly as he squeezed his wife's hand.

"Pleased to meet you, Jimmy. Thank you, I may take you up on your kind offer one of these days."

"To be sure, lassie. To be sure." His r's rolled delightfully over his tongue.

I stood. "I'll leave you two to catch up, but I would like to talk with you both later, if I may?"

Jimmy stood, while keeping Emma's tiny hand in his, loathe to ever let her go again, for any reason. "Miss Rellie, it would be an honor to assist you in whatever fine endeavor you choose. We look forward to further discussion." And he sat.

I was off in search of Etienne. This was becoming a disturbing habit, my actually seeking him out.

CHAPTER 18

Nothing went right for the next few days, either in Heaven or on Earth, in relation to The Case, as I'd begun to call it. Roger managed to elude the police and his fellow gang members, all the while escalating his stalking and emotional terrorizing of Rissa, hence, her entire family—including me. In turn, Etienne got no rest whatsoever from me.

Rissa, the strongest, most laid-back gal of her age that I knew, was a jangle of nerves and downright snippy. I remember when my darling daughter, Sara, got like that we said she was "in a snit." Rissa was most assuredly, and totally understandably, deep in the clutches of a royal snit. As a matter of fact, so was Sara. Alex and Wren weren't much better. Only Alex, Jr., away at computer camp, was spared the daily, moment-to-moment upheaval. Of course, he was as concerned as the rest of his family and frustrated he could not actually *be* there ... like me. The only difference was that an Amtrak train could not take *me* back to the family.

I was deeply touched by a conversation I heard between Rissa and her mother during this time of enforced togetherness, as they sat in the living room late one afternoon.

"I miss my Grams. I sometimes think it was all *my* fault that she died. If I hadn't asked for her special Florentine..." Rissa hung her head.

My heart flipped as Sara went over to her daughter and knelt beside the chair. "No, honey, please don't think like that. Grams had an *accident*. She certainly doesn't blame *you* for it, nor do I.

116

(Good for you, Sara. Right on, my dear. *I'm* the clumsy idiot with weak fingernails. Besides, it's pretty fine here. One day you'll see that for yourselves.)

Rissa bent down to hug her mother, before sighing and leaning back in the chair. "Thanks, Mom, but I wish I could see her just one more time."

"I know, so do I," Sara stood and walked back to the couch, where she sat, her back supported by a fluffy blue cushion.

"Why can't people come back, even for a moment?"

"Maybe they do. Some people think they do."

"What do *you* think, Mom?"

"I think...no, I *know*...your Grams loved us so very much that she is with us and still loving us, even if we can't see her. Love just doesn't go away like that."

"I hope that's really true, but I'd just like to *know*."

"Ah," Sara said.

"This is silly, Mom, but sometimes I ask her to give me a sign, like make a picture fall off the wall or my computer turn on by itself. Something. *Anything*." Rissa sat forward on the edge of the chair before placing her elbows on her knees. She looked so wonderfully young.

"Sweetie, it's not silly in the least. You loved her very much. It's a natural, normal wish. I've had it, too. I certainly miss my mother."

"I didn't mean to make you sad," Rissa said, as she arose from the chair.

Sara smiled. "I'm not sad. Thinking about her brings her closer."

"Good. I'm hungry!" Rissa headed for the kitchen.

(Oh, my lovely girls.)

***

Mister Robert continued to ponder the appropriate dispensation of the ring. His thinking became progressively muddled as each day's whiskey passed his lips. He ventured over to the corner of Sixth and Chestnut Streets every afternoon, in accordance with his former habit. Sorrow for the loss of his friend, Emma, washed over him every time. He accepted it as a penance for not helping her more successfully and for not being with her at the time of her death. He was convinced he had let her down. There was no one to console him, to tell him he had done his very best, and that she would understand. (She did.) The rest of the men he knew on the street clapped him on the back, said "too bad, but she's free of it now," and went shuffling on, never to mention her again.

During this hiatus from action, although I was not relaxed, it was a wonderful time to get acquainted with Pen, Seymour, Emma, and Jimmy, and to become reacquainted with Ian, all the while thrilled at the joy he and Thelma exhibited in each other. Without exception, all who knew of the situation with Rissa were both sympathetic and eager to offer whatever assistance they could to assure justice and safety. Emma's input on the movement of the local gangs was invaluable to us as we made our plans toward an Intervention of the complex variety.

Early one beautiful evening, we gathered on my backyard patio beneath a sunset a thousand times more spectacular than those I had once observed off Waikiki Beach in Honolulu, Hawaii.

"I've submitted the paperwork for a Complex Intervention," Pen said. "It takes time, but I stressed the need for a rush."

Etienne chuckled quietly. "Has anyone *ever* not wanted to rush into a Complex, Pen? The terms are synonymous, I believe."

"Right, but it doesn't hurt to request a rush just the same, Et, you know that."

"Keep the dander down, Pen-pen. You are right, as usual. It was simply an observation." Etienne the Calm.

Pen shook her head and muttered "Brothers!" as she glanced at the sunset with a sigh.

"How long does a rush Complex usually take?" I wanted, needed, to know.

"It can take up to a week. There's a lot to consider. It is the philosophy of Heaven that people on Earth should live as best they can, with what's available to them and what they can call up from within themselves. It is a learning experience down there, and a tough one at that," Pen answered.

"That's for sure, but ..."

"I think I know what you are going to say. But why, then, are there guardian angels, if folks are supposed to stumble about?"

I nodded my head. It would seem Etienne's entire family was psychic.

"Let me do this one," Etienne said.

"Do away, brother dear." Pen stood, bowed, and sat again.

"Thank you, thank you." He cleared his throat. I knew by now that throat clearing, when unnecessary, was Etienne's way of adding drama to a situation, of announcing the supposed import of his subsequent words. It was better than saying "Yo, listen up!" Not much, but better.

"Such an astute question deserves to be answered immediately," he smiled at me. Oh, those eyes. "Guardian angels are necessary to the large scheme of things. While it is patently true that Heaven wants folks to live life to the very best of each individual's ability by drawing on his or her talents and inner strengths, it is not a sink-or-swim type of affair in the least. Ideally, and Heaven is the origin and mainstay of idealism, a person will do as I've said all of the time. This, we know, is not true or even close to being true. SO ... enter guardian angels. We are provided to each person at the moment of birth to steer him or her in the proper direction, to intervene on an individual basis during the natural life span of the charge. It does not do for a person to succumb prematurely, hence, our main function is to literally help to keep our charges alive until the appropriate time. We do not interfere in all the little daily upheavals inherent in personhood. We'd be certifiable in a day if we attempted such a thing! It's amazing what people can tolerate. I've long admired human beings for their resilience and cleverness."

"Oh." I said.

"However," he continued, "every so often, a person needs something more than he or she realizes is already there inside themselves. The guardian angel can steer this person's thinking into the proper channels, so they think they've had a brilliant idea. Take gravity for instance. A G.A. had to literally hit Isaac Newton on the head with an apple to get him going properly. The invention of automobiles ushered in great challenges for G.A.s. It then became our additional responsibility to exert some control over possible accidents, that is, those that were not scheduled. Quite a mess, that job. It was far simpler when all we had to deal with were horses and chariots."

"You do digress, Etienne." This from Pen.

"Ah-hem, so I do," he cleared his throat again. "So, does that answer your question, Rellie?"

Oh, those eyes. And my birthmark was itching to beat the band. "Er, yes! Yes, I believe it does. Thanks."

"Is something wrong, Rellie?" Pen put her hand gently on my arm, as I continued to claw at my itch.

"No, it's just when I get nervous or worried, this damn birthmark drives me crazy!" I scratched some more.

"Let me see," she turned my arm toward her.

"OH MY GOSH! Etienne! Look at this! You won't believe this!"

Great, good. Now my mushroom/penis would be the talk of Heaven. Would I never escape the dratted thing?

Etienne stayed where he was and smiled.

"You *know* about this?" Pen was surprised.

"I was her G.A., of course I know about it," he snapped. "Now let's finish discussing The Case, shall we?"

I stood up. "No, let's finish discussing this, whatever it is. I want to know how come my birthmark is of such interest to your sister." I turned to Pen and raised my eyebrow. "Well?"

"Ah, it's an interesting shape, isn't it? Just like a pe-*mushroom*! Kinda cute, too." She giggled nervously.

"Mmmmm, no that's not it. Come on you two. What gives?" I'd noticed her slip of the tongue.

Etienne said, "Rellie, let's get everyone some iced herbal tea, shall we?" Without waiting for my reply, he gently took my elbow (the one without the birthmark) and walked me into my kitchen. The conversation hummed comfortably behind us.

"What was *that* all about?" I folded my arms in front of my chest and tapped my foot in a nervous tattoo on the blue tile floor. I believe there was a bit of a glare on my face as well.

"Sit down a minute, Debarelle, if you please."

Debarelle? Shit, this must be serious. Maybe it was a penis after all and not a mushroom?

We sat at the counter on my cushioned barstools. Etienne rolled up his left sleeve. Was he going to duke it out with me? "Look." He turned his elbow toward me.

There, perched in the exact same spot as my birthmark was an identical one of his own. I could hardly believe my eyes. It was shaped like a mushroom and looked, for all the world, exactly like mine. How could that be? "Are G.A.s marked the same as their charges?" I asked. "That's amazing and just like mine."

He smiled such a beatific smile that I could almost see sunbeams stream from his eyes. "No, we aren't marked. I find it utterly interesting that I should lo … like you so totally and be marked in the same way. It is truly Kismet, you do know that don't you?"

"Get a grip. I know nothing of the kind. Just as there must be a snowflake identical to another somewhere, there are birthmarks that match. It's not cosmic, it's simply coincidence." I stood. "Don't get all misty about it, Etienne."

In his disconcerting way, he ignored me yet riveted me in place with his eyes. I was drowning, clutching at straws. "When you were a baby, all shiny and newborn, that was the first thing I noticed, your birthmark. That is, after I made sure you were a girl, as I'd requested."

Good grief.

"My own birthmark had caused me no small bit of embarrassment as I grew up, just as yours did for you. I think I may have had just a tad more of a problem than you did with it, though."

"I doubt it, I really doubt it," I grumbled.

"No, think about it. I was a *boy*. We both know what the darned thing resembles. I can't tell you the number of times I was taunted about the one on my elbow being bigger than my other one!"

The devil made me do it, I swear. "Was it?"

"Not even when I was an infant!" He huffed and stood. The discussion was, quite obviously, over. "Let's rejoin our friends. I can see you are not in the proper frame of mind for such musings and mystifications." He didn't wait for me, but stomped off to the patio.

I remained behind to make the iced herbal tea and to wonder at the fragility of Etienne's ego. And, also, to grin like crazy.

CHAPTER 19

For the next few days, things were close to "normal" for Rissa. She went to school and participated in the swim team relays and races, winning a first and third in free style. That all was not quite right became more obvious in reference to her social life. "I haven't got one!" she wailed.

"You've got a life … it can be social later, after that boy is caught and put away," her mother cautioned her.

Meanwhile, Rissa's friends continued to be welcome at her house, as were all of their friends. The rec room in the basement was still a favorite meeting spot for her and her friends, male and female. Everyone knew what had happened and supported her decision to testify against the boy. That is, once he was found.

The "normal" state of affairs changed one evening after Rissa said good-night to her friends, waving as they walked out the front door and down the front walk. "See you tomorrow!" and "Thanks, Rissa!" She closed the front door, locking the two original locks and the two new ones her mother had insisted a locksmith install the night following Roger's visit to Rissa's school. Because she was the last to go up to bed, she punched in the burglar alarm code before climbing the stairs. It had been a fun night, with so much laughter her stomach still hurt. She was lucky to have such fine friends.

When she reached the top of the stairs, she could hear her father's snores wafting out into the hallway. She smiled. How her mother could sleep next to such a racket, she had no idea. Had to be love. She could not remember a time, like some of her friends discussed about their parents, when hers ever slept apart unless one of them was off on a business trip. The older they got, the less they went on such trips. It was cool; they were okay having around. Especially now. She shuddered and went into her room at the end of the hallway. Because of its location over the garage, it was colder than her brothers' room in the winter. But she loved it; it was hers, and unlike Alex and Wren, she didn't have to share it.

Still smiling, Rissa reached instinctively around the door jamb as she entered her room and flipped the light switch that turned on her little bedside Tiffany lamp. She flung her shoes in two separate directions and one bounced off the wall under the back window. Rissa reached beneath the lamp for the small radio beside her bed. That's when she saw it; a note was stuck in the black plastic handle on the top of the radio. It was stuck there, waiting for her to enter her room and see it.

She sat on the edge of her bed, removed the note, unfolded it, and read with mounting horror: "I can get yu any time I wunt too. Lik the roome. Nice. Sweet dreems." She clutched the offending paper tightly in her hand and turned toward the window. Her curtains were closed, but she couldn't help wondering if he was out there watching her read his horrible note. Could he see her right now, this very minute? With a sick feeling in the pit of her stomach, she wondered how he had gotten in. When? If he could get in once, he could do so again, just like he said.

"Oh, God!" Her hand went to her mouth and she bit down hard on her thumb. "That son of a bitch! Damn him! I wish he were the dead one, not that nice lady. Why'd I ever have to go on that class trip? Why couldn't I have been sick that day? Why didn't I go to Tower Records and the Gallery Mall and all those places Jamie wanted to visit? Why was I such a little doo-bee. 'Let's visit Congress Hall,' I said. Shit, shit, shit!" She threw the note across the room and punched her pillow.

"What's going on in there, honey? Are you all right?"

"Yes, no ... Mom, come on in, I have something to show you."

✳✳✳

Roger was miles away, sitting at the bar at Jake's, by the time his note caused the precise reaction he'd wanted. It had been ridiculously easy getting inside that little cunt's room tonight. He'd watched the house for a few nights and gotten a good feel for the family's routine. They had a storage shed in the far corner of their back yard, which provided him the cover required for the stakeouts. There was a little creek behind the property and tall grasses grew along its edge. It was perfect for his purposes. A pair of stolen binoculars assisted him in his endeavor.

The family's pathetic, little routine was boringly the same each week night. Daddy arrived home; Mommy was in the kitchen. They cooked dinner together and seemed to enjoy it. Meanwhile, a kid who looked just like his mother, blared rock music from his bedroom window at the right rear of the house. Actually, his music wasn't bad. Okay, so that was the kid's room. So it wasn't Marissa's room. The family actually sat together and ate dinner with each other at a frickin' table. They didn't use their fingers and no one, not a one, threw food or beer cans. All of their drinks were in *glasses*, for chrissake. They talked to each other; no one hollered or stormed out of the house. Then, holy shit, they each helped clean up afterwards, all at the same time, still laughing and talking. What the hell did they have to talk so much about? It sure took them a long time just to eat dinner, like a half hour or more.

His observations showed him that every night one of two things happened: either they all stayed home where they read, talked, laughed, watched television, visited with friends who came by, or, on other nights after dinner, they all went out some where, to return two or three hours later. The only difference was the boy, who sometimes stayed home alone. Big deal, Roger could care less about that kid. Once, another boy showed up and slept in the same room with the kid. Fag friend? Brother? Who gave a fuck.

They locked up at the same time every night, turned their lights out at the same time every night, and activated their alarm at the same time each and every night when everyone stayed home after dinner. They were Schedule People, real tight asses these people. That made his caper as easy as pie. When little darling daughter had her friends over, there was another schedule: brother escaped to his room; parents went to theirs a few hours later. So, the old folks slept in the room at the front of the house. That meant the room over the garage was his target.

He quickly realized he could get inside most easily as the family sat down to dinner, when they were relaxed and talking up a storm. No alarms were on that early in the evening. Someone had even had the forethought to hang a rose trellis on the garage wall directly beneath the girl's window. He couldn't believe it. They spend an effing fortune on security and the dipshits leave a virtual *ladder* to the sacrosanct room of the little virgin darling! He almost wet himself laughing over that one.

Roger was seated at the end of the bar nearest the pool table, pouring his fifth beer down his throat, as he remembered climbing up that trellis, pushing up the unlocked window with ease, and falling into the room onto soft blue carpet. He could hear the family downstairs, hooting it up over some stunt the kid had pulled during his Boy Scout trip the year before. *Boy Scouts?* It figures. Next thing they'd be standing up to sing "America The Beautiful." Knowing he should rush, he still took the time to scan the room and open her dresser drawers to remove a pair of red silk bikini panties. He'd shoved them into his pocket, left the note, and climbed back down to the yard. No one saw him; it was clean. It was perfect.

"Do it again, Jake." He slammed his empty mug onto the scratched surface of the old stained wooden bar.

"Take it easy, Rog. If you didn't have me by the shorties, you'd not be served. You're only sixteen." Nonetheless, Jake placed a full mug of tap in front of Roger. "You gotta pay for it, at least, you know," he growled.

"Yeah, yeah. My luck I was there when you was comin' outta that jewelry store with a bag all done up like Santy Claus, right Jake-o? Never said nothin' neither, have I? Just keep bein' nice to me and I never will," he winked at Jake and took a long drink of the ice-cold beer.

"Just keep that soda bottle beside that beer there," Jake reminded him. "If the pigs even walk past the door, man, pick it up and pretend someone else left the brew behind. Got it?"

"I know the drill, Jake. I ain't stupid."

Jake wasn't too sure about that, but he knew enough to keep quiet. A part-time petty crook, he had respect for people organized enough to be in a gang, even if it was some little punk still dripping behind the ears. He only ripped off jewelry stores now and then, to liven things up. Running a bar was a good living, but ever so boring. Besides, every time he got himself a new old lady, he had to give her presents. They all wanted jewelry, the real shit. When they broke up with him, as they always did, not one of those broads ever offered to give back any of the fancy stuff he'd bestowed upon them. Dames!

"Besides," Jake added, "the cops are thicker than flies on warm shit today. Every five minutes they come in here askin' for you."

"*Me*? What they want me for?" Roger's entire body tensed.

"Said you killed some old bag lady, Rog."

"*Killed* an old lady? Me? I wouldn't do a thing like that, Jake. You know that!" What were the cops trying to do, trick him? Well, he didn't trick so easy, man.

"Said she died last Friday over at the hospital. What do you know about this?"

"Jake, you're one nosy son of a bitch, you are. You should know by now to keep your snoozer outta what's got nothin' to do with ya."

"I worry about you, Rog. You're my favorite little asshole!" Jake laughed and turned the volume up on the ballgame on the television in the corner near the register.

"And you're my favorite dick, but what's that gotta do with the day's crop of crap?" He finished the beer. "Gimme another, gotta take a piss. Be right back." He stumbled from the barstool.

Once in the filthy restroom, one hand supporting himself on the damp wall behind the urinal, Roger peed. Dead? The old broad *died*? Was that possible? Hell, sure it was, a fucking car just about ran over the dishrag. But, who cares? She was only a bag lady, for chrissake! Wait an effing minute. The cops were tryin' to flush him out, that's probably all it was.

He flushed the toilet and went to the vomit-encrusted sink to toss a little water onto his face. What a scum hole this place was, but it was the only place he was served without a big hassle. He felt dizzy and leaned his forehead against the damp, chipping green plaster on the walls. The cops. Yeah, they circulated that story to get people to rat on good old Roger. Pretty soon, a reward would be offered for information leading to his arrest. His ass was grass once that happened. He couldn't think of one person who wouldn't hop onto that bandwagon. Hell, there'd be a long line right behind his miserable bitch of a mother! He shook his head. He had to think. Too much beer. No, not enough beer. He'd have another and think this thing out. He shoved open the restroom door and returned to the barstool. A fresh beer awaited him beside the now-warm bottle of soda.

Neither Jake nor Roger gave much thought to the disheveled old man who staggered into the middle booth. He slouched down in the seat, barely upright, and propped himself in the corner. He appeared to go to sleep, but was actually as alert as he had ever been in his life. He was not sober, not by a long shot, but he was not yet drunk. His mind was going a mile a minute, his heart rate had increased to its maximum exercise rate while he was sitting still. The man smiled as he caressed the sharp blade in his pocket; it would do the trick.

Mister Robert had found Roger.

CHAPTER 20

*E*arlier in the day, Mister Robert had buried Emma's ring near the war memorial in Washington Square Park. He had done it before the sun was up, before anyone was around to watch, wait, then dig it right back up and put it into their pocket to pawn later for drugs or booze. He vowed that Emma's ring would not end up like that.

He had dug behind the memorial wall, using a flattened Pepsi can he'd found in the middle of Spruce Street. When the hole was a foot deep, he stopped. He removed the ring from his pocket, kissed it fondly, wrapped it in the pretty piece of giftwrap he had found inside a trash can on Market Street, and gently placed the bundle into the center of the hole. After covering it up and tapping the dirt down, he pulled up some grass and sprinkled it onto the fresh dirt, making it appear, at quick glance, as if nothing had been disturbed.

Mister Robert went away for thirty minutes to visit behind the same floral shop where he had gotten the flowers to take to Emma in the hospital. He found slim pickings, but managed to get two yellow roses with perhaps another three hours' bloom in them. As he walked back to the park, he gathered a decent crop of dandelions and buttercups to add to the mix. He first placed the cobblestone he had worked loose in the alley behind Congress Hall atop the makeshift "grave," then he positioned the flowers. Sitting back on his heels in the moist dirt and grass, Mister Robert sent a prayer to Heaven for Emma. He hoped it would be heard, not because he said it (he was unsure of his credibility there), but because it was for such a fine lady.

He got up with some difficulty, brushed the knees of his threadbare trousers off as best he could, sat on a bench nearby, and pulled the half-pint of bourbon from his jacket pocket. That's when he saw what he thought was the punk kid who had killed Emma, so he followed him, pretending to be more than a tad inebriated. He felt safe in the knowledge that he was beneath the kid's notice.

As he sat in the darkness of the booth in Jake's Bar, Mister Robert awaited his opportunity. He had already decided he would kill Roger, stabbing him with the knife he'd found at the bottom of the trash can behind the floral shop. It had seemed a lucky omen finding that knife while getting flowers for Emma's "grave." Until that moment, Mister Robert had had no idea how he was going to remove Roger from the face of the Earth. The murder of Roger had become an atonement in his mind, a great deed to memorialize Emma's goodness, and to assuage his own feelings of inadequacy.

✳✳✳

"Danger, danger!" The horns beeped inside the Guardian Angel administrative office of Grand G.A. Helga.

"Drat! That always happens when I'm on duty!" She hurried over to the massive electronic board to locate the source of trouble. "Ah, just as I suspected, sector four thousand and eighteen. Lots of trouble there lately." She shrugged her shoulders, "If not there, it'd be somewhere, so I guess it might as well be there."

Helga went to the pager, pushed sixteen buttons, and returned to her desk. Retrieving her current romance novel, she found the page she had been reading before being interrupted. She read while awaiting the arrival of those paged.

She did not have long to wait. G.A.s were prompt. They had to be; timing was paramount in their profession. Quickly enter-

ing her office were Etienne, Pen, Seymour (with extreme reluc-
tance), and Carstairs. Joining them were Felicia (Wren's G.A.);
Laura (Alex Jr.'s), Mulligan (Sara's), Arlene (Alex's), Sam (Jamie's),
and Paul (Mister Robert's) as well as six administrative board members. These would make a quorum, if an emergency vote were
necessary.

By the time everyone had taken his or her seat in the meeting
room outside Helga's office, she had received a detailed report
over the fax. This she carried into the room, seating herself at the
desk facing the others.

"What's going on?" Seymour asked. "Why was I dragged out
at this hour?"

"This hour," Helga consulted her watch, "is four o'clock in
the afternoon, Seymour. Did our crisis interrupt your afternoon
snooze?" No one laughed. They were as curious as was Seymour
why he was involved with this particular group, considering his
resignation in good standing from Roger's guardianship.

Helga pushed her chair aside and stood behind the desk while
she read the report: "The alarm has been sent by Paul, who as you
know, is Mister Robert's G.A. Paul has been extremely concerned
about his charge since Emma's accident and subsequent demise.
He has returned to his drinking, but it is his emotional condition
that most worries Paul at this juncture. We have been informed
that Mister Robert has taken it upon himself to remove Roger
from everyone's hair, so to speak. Earlier today, he found a knife
and has followed Roger to a bar, where he is now awaiting an
opportunity to strike. Paul, now that you are here with us, please
fill us in."

Paul did so, starting with the burial of the ring and the finding of the knife to Mister Robert's current position in the dark
booth in Jake's Bar. "I am quite concerned about this, because I
understand a Complex Intervention has been applied for and permission is pending as we speak." We all nodded in the affirma-

tive. "Because that's the case, I must restrain my charge as best I can, because so many others are involved at this point." He again glanced around the room. "Each of you has the responsibility of guarding one of the principals in this drama. I cannot let a loose cannon alter the Intervention."

"Why not?" I asked. "Just let Mister Robert loose and all of our problems would be solved nice and neatly." What was the matter with these people?

Five voices started at once.

Helga's voice was the loudest. "Okay, one at a time! Etienne, she's your problem, you handle it."

"What? I'm not a prob..." I was incensed.

"Rellie, ah, let me explain this to you." Etienne pulled his chair closer to mine. His voice, as usual, was soft and unhurried. His eyes ... oh, my lord. His eyes were so *deep*, so beautiful. Why'd he have to have such eyes, for shits' sake.

"Rellie, you're not thinking clearly." I started to speak, but he raised his hand. "No, you're not, and it is completely understood by all in this room. This situation has touched you deeply; your granddaughter and her family have become heavily involved. You are, quite naturally, very worried. This has, I'm afraid, clouded your head."

Okay, so he was right. I grimaced and nodded.

"What cannot happen is for Mister Robert to kill Roger. If that should happen, we have only removed the tip of the iceberg, so to speak. Even though we now know Roger is *persona non grata* with Juan and the other members of the Hellraiser gang, as well as with his brother's little hoods, neither group can afford to loose "face" and will, most assuredly, retaliate should Roger end up dead. Their convoluted philosophy says it's perfectly fine for them to kill each other, but don't let an outsider do it. Think how much worse that could be for Rissa and the others. No, Paul must immediately run a Simple Intervention past Mister Robert, while we await the approval of our Complex." He nodded to Paul. "If I am correct, Seymour is here as a courtesy, because he is Roger's former GA, but he need not be involved in Paul's Intervention."

"That is absolutely right, Etienne. You do understand, Rellie?" Paul asked not unkindly.

"I guess so. But it's a good thing I'm not down there while this is going on, or you guys would have a BIG task on your hands keeping me from personally strangling that little punk."

Etienne sighed. "Good thing you're here, then." *That* made the others chuckle. Not me.

Paul left the meeting immediately to get started on his Simple Intervention for Mister Robert. Helga left us, returning to her desk by the electronic board to resume reading her novel. The others discussed the best plan for the Complex Intervention, while I sat there stewing with frustration, because I could only wait for it all to come together. I was a new arrival without much experience, one who was not supposed to participate in an Intervention. But I would be involved; I'd give 'em my ideas and suggestions; I'd … wait and worry.

As I sat listening to the discussion, the machinations and plans to help Rissa, I realized how special guardian angels were and how wonderful to have been blessed with one, even if it was Etienne. That each of us, while on Earth, is assigned a G.A. is such a gift. A G.A.'s job is an awesome responsibility. Several hours later, when the meeting was concluded, I left with a healthy respect for G.A.s and their work. Even Etienne looked better, much better. The rascal must have sensed something had changed within me, because he dazzled me with one of his best smiles. I felt better than I had in a long, long time. With this crew's help, things *had* to work out all right.

I resolved then and there to enroll in G.A. School the very second I could. Naturally, I had no inkling how my plans would irrevocably change.

CHAPTER 21

*R*oger was undeniably drunk, twizzled, fou, smashed. Jake had flagged him, so there'd be no more drinks today.

"Sure, okay, man," he said, as he stumbled out the door into bright sunshine. He hated coming out of a bar into daylight. The world was buzzin' around, people were laughin' and enjoyin' themselves, and all he had comin' was a hangover. It was like his life was over, while everyone else was havin' a great time. He hated that. He didn't notice the raggedly dressed man following him as he headed for some shade, a place to sleep off the beer. He had to think; he had to find out the truth about that bag broad, if she was really dead or not. He'd rest a bit and that'd be the next thing he'd do after that. He needed a nap, was all. Once it was dark he'd feel a hell of a lot better. Daytime was the pits, man. Nighttime, that was where it was at, nothin' worthwhile you couldn't do at night and do easier than in the light, for sure.

Mister Robert stayed on the other side of the street, walking in the same direction as Roger. This way, he figured it would not appear that he was following the boy. As he walked, he slid the knife from his pocket, keeping it hidden in his hand with the hilt shoved under the sleeve of his shirt and the blade held carefully in the palm of his hand. He followed Roger through the park and, when he turned south on Fifth Street, he crossed the street. Now he was on the same side as Roger. When they got to South Street, Mister Robert realized he was not able to keep up with the drunken kid. He watched as Roger gained distance, but he gamely tried to keep up. When the kid stopped to take a leak against the side wall of the Tower Classical Records store, Mister Robert caught up.

At the moment he was ready to make his move against Roger, Mister Robert tripped. What amazed him was that he had tripped over exactly nothing, nothing at all except plain old flat sidewalk. There wasn't even a pebble in sight. It felt like someone had pushed him; he'd even turned around to give the person "what for," but no one was there. It was the most incredible thing. Even when he was drunk, which he was not now, he'd never done such a thing. Dazed but unhurt, he pushed himself up, dusted himself off, and scratched his head. That was one weird event.

(At the moment, his guardian angel, Paul, was smiling a very self-satisfied smile as he left the Simple Intervention area. "Well done!" his fellow G.A.s said. "It's always the simplest thing that does the trick, isn't it?" he grinned.)

When Mister Robert looked, Roger was out of sight. There was no indication in which direction he had gone. South Street was a busy area any time of the day or night. There was no sign of the kid. "Damn!" he muttered. "Might as well have a drink," he said to himself. "Bad pennies inevitably turn up sooner or later."

After retrieving the knife from a broken section of the sidewalk, he carefully placed it into the torn pocket of his equally torn jacket, picked up a quarter hidden in the grass, started off down South Street, and was caught up in the *joie de vivre* always on display there.

✳✳✳

It was dark when Roger awoke, curled in a tight ball behind a trash bin along Delaware Avenue. It was a starless night, and there was a chill in the spring air. He could hear voices and laughter coming from Katmandu, the club nearest his spot. The lights around the outside dancing area and bars were twinkling in the darkness and looked festive. Roger hated that, too. It seemed everyone belonged somewhere. Now he didn't even have the gang to hang with since they'd black-balled him.

Standing shakily, he spit into the river behind him before going out onto the roadway. He wanted back into the Hellraisers; they were the best there was, but he would have to avoid Juan for the time being, until he could prove Emma was better and back doing what she did best—absolutely nothing. What a waste of space that bitch was! If she really had died, so effin' what? But he'd better check it out, 'cause cops looked at things a lot differently than he did, that was for sure.

As he walked, he decided to go over to the hospital. The direct approach, that's what. He'd saunter in and ask about his poor, mentally impaired auntie, how was she? No, he couldn't stay right now, he had a meetin,' but he would be back when he had more time to spend with her.

Without looking, he walked directly into the path of an oncoming car whose driver was alert and angry, evident from his gestures out the window. "Suck this!" Roger returned the gestures. The driver continued on, and so did Roger. "Muh-fuh!" he grumbled.

The near miss had awakened a part of Roger's brain that had been on holiday. He smacked himself in the forehead. "Idiot! Man, you are so stupid it's a wonder you can find your nose to pick it!"

He sat on the curb in front of a drugstore in Head House Square near Lombard Street. There was no way he could walk up to that hospital, go in, and start asking questions about that dame. No way, man! If she'd croaked as rumor had it, the cops'd either be there or have a bulletin out for him if he showed his face. They'd be lookin' for anyone asking questions about that broad.

He was temporarily screwed, but only temporarily. Think … think…He had it! He'd call the hospital and give them the same routine he'd conceived for the in-person visit, while remaining safely out of sight.

That is precisely what he did after making sure there were no police drifting around the phone booth area to cause him trouble. Naturally, the phone book had been forcibly removed from the booth. That always irritated Roger. What a lame thing to do. Why bother with such small, nowhere shit? Phone books couldn't be pawned or traded. Stupid-ass kids. All it was, was damned inconvenient.

Roger got the hospital's phone number from the robot at "5-5-5" and made the call. The receptionist who answered asked his name and he said, "Father Patrick O'Leary." He got a kick out of that name. Patrick O'Leary had been the first kid he'd cut with a blade (the little souvenir knife his brother Wayne had nicked for him while in Atlantic City) back in the fifth grade. The idiot had tried to get in front of him in line for a Good Humor popsicle. All the kids knew Roger got to go first, every time, without fail. One day, Patrick mistakenly thought *he* could go first. Think again, little prick. There'd been so many kids hanging around the truck that day that no one could prove Roger had done it, and no one tried. Patrick's mother was dead from a car accident and his father didn't go home until he was drunk enough to forget it. Patrick had to fend for himself as best he could. He knew he was no match for Roger. Besides, it was just a little puncture wound on his shoulder.

The receptionist at the hospital's main desk said all she could tell him was that Emma was no longer at the hospital. "She may have checked out," she suggested, "I'll have to check that for you, Father. I'm new here, just started yesterday. If you don't mind holding?"

"No, fine. I'll hold," he said. "I'll wait, but I have this meetin' at the church and can't wait too long." He was pretty certain when she said "checked out" it didn't mean what he meant by it. He sure as hell hoped not.

Roger was not good at waiting. He tapped his fingers on the shelf; double-checked to see if any coins had been forgotten in the little coin return slot (they had not); and experienced several nervous minutes as he watched a black and white turn the corner and slow down next to the booth. His fingers turned white on the phone before he realized both cops were busy checking out a South Street whore bent over to talk to a john in his car, her tits on display for the dude, her ass catching the breezes and the cops' eyes. The cops drove on, turning at the next corner. If they were cruising around the block, he couldn't stay here. Besides, the broad who'd asked him to hold could have started a trace. "Hello?" he called into the frustratingly quiet receiver. "Hello? Where the hell's everybody?"

Several seconds of silence ensued, and then he heard, "Father?" She sounded out of breath.

"Yeah, what's goin' on? Is she okay or what?" He was impatient.

"I'm not supposed to give this information over the phone, Father, unless you're a member of the family, but since you're a priest, I can tell you she did not check out, she ..."

He interrupted her. The scumbucket broad wasn't dead! Relief turned his bones to water and greatly improved his manners. "Bless you, ma'am. She *is* gettin' better then?"

"Oh, dear ... ah, not exactly, Father. I'm sorry to tell you, she passed away. I'm so sorry ..."

He left the phone swinging from its wire-covered cord and erupted from the booth, snapping a hinge on the folding door in the process. The bitch really had checked out, just like Jake said. Because she'd gone and done that, he was in deeper shit than he'd ever been in during his entire miserable life. He would have to hide out better than he'd been doing, but first he needed to pay another visit to that little girl, Marissa, out in the 'burbs. It was essential she keep her big mouth firmly shut. He would have to convince her of that one way or another. He didn't want to have to kill her, but he was already wanted for one murder, could another make much difference, if he were caught?

Roger was a tough kid, but faced with Emma's death and his complicity in it, he was only too aware it spelled a murder rap. And that scared him for the second time in his life. He remembered the first time when he'd been a dumb little kid and thought his father would never stop hitting him in the head one night because he'd wet his pants after falling down the concrete steps out front of their tenement and split his lip open. That's the night he promised no one would ever hurt him again, and he wouldn't ever be scared any more. Wrong.

CHAPTER 22

*I*t was past midnight when Roger parked the bicycle behind some bushes in the area behind Marissa's house. He'd made no special plans other than to scare the shit out of her. He knew the cops would have called her family as soon as the bag lady died. They'd want the girl's testimony now more than ever. To get it, they'd have to keep her feeling safe so she'd continue to be talkative. Roger could not allow that to happen.

The night was cool and the air smelled damp, clouds moved rapidly across the face of the near-full moon and resembled witches flying about on broomsticks. The leaves in the trees rustled and branches scraped together, creating a mournful sound. The crickets had stopped singing. Roger heard a dog whimper farther down the block as a nearby cat fight increased in volume and intensity. He smiled, you could almost hear them spit. By morning there would be a tell-tale area of fur lying on the lawn. The cat fight was good; it made him homesick for the gang, even Juan the Prick. No one pushed the Hellraisers around, no one came into their territory, unless they were looking for a fight or to get hurt. Roger continued to listen as the cat fight escalated. Those cats, they were all right. Maybe they'd fight to the death. Yeah. Survival of the fittest, man.

The floodlights were like beacons surrounding her house. In the growing fog, the house looked eerily like a giant spaceship filled with alien beings who moved about only in the dark of night.

Roger shook his head. "Geesh! I'm in the 'burbs where it's as boring as watching squirrel shit dry and I'm getting' the heebie-jeebies. Nothing like the city, man, that's where it's *at*."

He knew the state-of-the-art alarm system her pappy had installed after his last visit to Saint Marissa's bedroom would be primed and ready to announce his smallest movement toward the sacred castle. He'd been riding along her street the day an Alarm-It Company truck was parked in the driveway. Alarm-It was famous for hi-tech, state-of-the-art intruder alarms. There was no way he would get near the little bitch this night. But he could watch a while. Maybe she would lean out of her window and sense his presence. He could rise up from the fog like a monster and really pucker her little pink asshole. He chuckled.

He leaned against a tree to take a leak as he glanced up at her bedroom window. He'd been in that room where she would lie all soft and pink on her comfortable mattress with her pastel sheets, her long, dark hair freed from its pigtail and spread over the pillow like a silken waterfall, her eyes closed in sleep, her soft lips parted slightly. His penis swelled in his hand; it became hard as a steel beam. How he'd love to creep into that room and slide between her warm virginal thighs. He remained in the shadows, stroking himself to the accompaniment of his lascivious thoughts.

✳✳✳

They were waiting for him when he rode the bike across Delaware Avenue three hours later. The clouds continued to thicken. The air smelled of impending rain. Juan and Mike were on him before he realized they were there. Man! He'd lost his touch. It was all that old dame's fault for dyin' and causin' him so much trouble. He didn't say a word, just stood there, after leaning the bike against the stone abutment of the highway. He crossed his arms in front of his chest, not knowing it was a defensive action, one people often assumed when feeling threatened.

"The hero has arrived," Juan sneered as he stepped closer. Mike followed faithfully behind and attempted a sneer of his own, which fell short and resembled more the face of someone with severe diarrhea in an area with no facilities.

"Hello, Juan, how are ya?" Roger didn't move, his face remained blank.

"Cut the crap, boyo. That street meat broad *died*, man. You are in deep shit, Rog-baby." Juan leaned toward Roger as he spoke, invading Roger's space, making him even more uncomfortable, but he held his ground, muscles primed for a quick dodge of a fist.

"Yeah, she croaked. B-F-D!" No sense showing Juan how nervous this fact made him.

"It *is* a big fuckin' deal, Rogie." Juan poked his index finger into Roger's chest. Damn finger felt like the hard metal bore of a gun. "You are now wanted for murder. A thing like that could kill you." He laughed at his sorry joke.

Inwardly wincing, Roger tried to maintain his bravado. "Yeah, guess I'm pretty important now, huh? Is there a reward for me now? Is that why you guys are here, to turn me over for the money?"

"YOU STUPID SHIT! When brains were handed out, yours were trampled by elephants first. Of course we'd want the money, but there isn't any. Besides, you're not smart enough to avoid capture long enough to be worth anything in the way of cash."

"Now just a minute. I don't have to stand here and be insulted!" He uncrossed his arms and made fists of his hands, as he let them swing threateningly, he hoped, by his sides.

"Sure you do," Juan said with a slick smile. "Want to know why?" Roger remained silent. "Since you asked so nicely, I'll tell you. We can't have that little girl out in the 'burbs blabbin' all about the Hellraisers, it could give us a bad rep." Juan laughed so hard, Roger thought he would vomit. Mike echoed each guffaw. "We thought we'd find us a nice car and take us a little ride out to those pretty 'burbs, have us a little chat with that girlie. But, yo!

We'll plan it later, it's Thursday, man, another booze and pussy night comin' on, the unofficial start of another weekend of fun and games. We'll go Monday afternoon, when she's home from school. We thought you should come along with us."

This was obviously not an invitation. Roger recognized he had no choice. It sounded as if Juan and the boys wanted to actually *help* him. What was the catch? These were not nice people, that's why Roger liked them so much, but they were up to something and that could prove to be most unpleasant for him.

"Sure, Juan. Great idea. What's the catch?"

"You've grown some balls since our last conversation, I see. Nice ones, right Mike?" Mike grinned. "Guess you'll want to keep 'em, huh, Rog?" Roger nodded. "Then be a good boy and do as you're told." He poked twice more into Roger's chest. It was all Roger could do to remain standing.

"Okay, Juan. Whatever you say, you're the boss."

"HOT DAMN! Mike, did you hear that? Music to my poor ears. Our Roger has wised up!" He threw his arms around Roger's shoulders and squeezed.

"Okay, Juan. It's good to see ya, but what's goin' on here, really?"

"Sit your sorry ass down and I'll tell you," Juan sat on the curb and pat a dirty spot beside him. Roger sat. Mike, unsure what to do, hovered behind Juan until he was told to "take a walk" for an hour. Pouting, he left.

"Roger, the truth is, we were all angry before. I didn't want the cops crawlin' after us, accusin' us of all sorts of things we've probably done a thousand times. It's a nuisance, disturbs our business, you know? Sure you do. But, Roger, you're one of us, a *Hellraiser*. Ain't nothin' better. When you were busy bein' a pain in the ass about pushin' that sack of crap into the street, I had to get you away to give us all time to cool down, to give the cops one person to look for, not the entire gang. Unnerstand?"

"Yeah, Juan. You left me to the cops."

"No, no, no. Roger, you miss the point, as usual." He pat Roger on the back. "I felt, that is, we all felt, you stood a better chance out there on your own than with us. But now that's changed. There's safety in numbers now the broad's dead."

"Safety for you, you mean, don't you Juan?" Roger figured he was in trouble already, why not make it worse?

"What are you talkin' about, buddy?" Juan's voice threatened.

Roger stood up, began pacing, again ready to jump out of Juan's way if necessary. "I'm talkin' about you're not helpin' me when I needed it. I'm talkin' about you desertin' me, kickin' me out. I'm talkin' about now the baggie is dead, it's a murder rap. I'm talkin' about how if *I* go down, *you* go down, Juan. You were the other one with me that day, remember? That's what's behind this oh-so-friendly shit, isn't it? You want to save your own ass, not mine."

Shaking his head, Juan stood and walked over to Roger. "It hurts me to the bone, to my very soul, to hear you talk like that, Roger. You're a Hellraiser. I love you, man!"

"Give me a break." Roger stepped away from Juan.

"Okay, so I shouldn't have sent you away. I know that now. You're right, we're in this together. One thing you got to remember: it was *you* did the pushin.' I just stole the girlie's little bitty purse. Speakin' of which, how'd you get ahold of those credit cards and license? I know it was you."

"Yeah, so what? You weren't helpin' me, and I had to find her address and stuff."

"Doesn't matter, it was smart of you, makes me proud of your resourcefulness."

"Juan cut the crap!" Roger started to walk away, totally fed up.

"Roger? You want it fresh?"

"Yeah, for a change." He turned to look at Juan, but made no move closer.

"Fact is, you have made the Hellraisers famous around here. It was somethin' even *I* had not foreseen."

At last Roger understood. "Ah-ha! Now you need me, is that it? So you can brag about how tough the Hellraisers are now that murder is part of the mix. Go kill your own person." He turned to walk away.

Juan grabbed him by the arm, less roughly than usual. "It's not my bag, Rog. We're all so proud of you. It was not somethin' I was aware would happen, but all by yourself you have made a real name for us, a *real* name. We are the primo gango now, my friend!" Juan flashed him a big smile. "The other thing is, well, we're bored out of our eff'n skulls with the penny-ante shit we've grown used to. Roger, you might not believe it, but we are all so good at what we do, there ain't too many challenges left for our clever brains. Helpin' you, who has made the Hellraiser rep for all time, would be excitin'."

This was incredible, thought Roger. Here was Juan, tough man without a heart, acknowledging someone else was necessary to the Hellraisers. What was more, Juan was willing to help him beat this thing, albeit to preserve and maintain the new tenuous hold the Hellraisers had on top billing, thereby polishing his image as their leader. It would also keep Juan's dick outta the wringer, save his sorry ass from an accessory to murder charge. No small benefit. Yes, incredible … and useful one day soon, he would make certain of it. Perhaps he could take over the leadership if the others thought he'd go to another gang, enhancing the other gang's rep a hundred-fold. He'd see about that. Meanwhile, he'd play along.

"Okay, Juan. It feels good to be back, man. We'll go see that little girl after school on Monday like you said." He put out his hand; Juan shook it and grinned. "Hot damn! Let's have ourselves some fun, dude!"

***

Mister Robert went unobserved by the two scheming young men under the highway. He had been looking for a place to sleep out of the wind and impending rain, when he saw Roger ride his bicycle across Delaware Avenue. As he paused, not wanting to be seen and scare the boy away, Mister Robert observed two young men who appeared to be following Roger. Cautiously, Mister Robert made his way across the trash-strewn sidewalk and positioned himself so he could watch what looked like a meeting.

After what appeared to be an agreement between two of the young men, the third having left or been banished before the hollering began, the two walked away chatting like old friends. That's when he decided to follow. That's when he found the enemy's lair, the gang's hideout under the bridge farther down the street. The two had gone there, joined up with some others, and were drinking, when Mister Robert silently left, heading for the police station where Rissa had originally given her statement.

✳✳✳

Otis had been missing from the gang for a good (translate: bad) reason—he'd been in jail. They'd told him it was because he was drunk, as indeed he was, with a .19 blood-alcohol level (in Pennsylvania .10 is legal intoxication). Once they had him locked up, they started on him about Roger. Where was he, and that kind of shit. Otis had no idea where he was and told that to the cops. Even if he had known where Roger was every second of every day, he wouldn't have told the cops. He could tell they didn't believe him, but what could they do? It was ironic. It was the first time Otis had ever told a cop the truth, and they didn't believe him.

His headache was immense and his stomach felt horrible. His very guts rumbled and cramped so badly he could barely walk out of the cell. But he did it. He'd rather blow up and die outside the joint than give the boys in blue the opportunity to watch him suffer.

As he slowly made his way, ever so carefully (his head just might fall off if he rushed things), down the stone stairs outside the police building, he had time to see a shabbily dressed old man slowly make his way up the steps and pass within four feet of him. Otis stopped and turned, as did the old man. Their eyes met before each turned to continue his journey in the opposite direction.

Had they but known it, their thoughts were connected.

"That looked like one of those Hellraiser boys, one of the Bad Ones Emma feared so much. I'm sure I've seen that kid with Roger."

"I wonder what that sack o' bones could want inside? He didn't look too swift, maybe he was turning himself in for being stupid." Otis laughed. "You know, he did look familiar. Like I've seen him before somewheres."

✳✳✳

They had been debating and planning for four hours nonstop and had finally arrived at what they felt to be a workable plan for the Complex Intervention. There were a few holes that needed plugging, but all agreed it could work.

"Shouldn't we have heard from the committee by now?" I asked. "Does it usually take this long to get approval? Do they ever disapprove a Complex?" My voice rose in fear.

Etienne, who had remained by my side throughout the entire meeting, pat me on the shoulder and answered quietly, "Yes."

Somewhat used to his seemingly cryptic responses, I, for once, did not get unnerved. I asked calmly, "And that answer applies to which question?"

"Yes to all three, Rellie."

I could not sustain my ire for long. "For Heaven's sake, Etienne! You act as if there's a premium on words around here, as if you'll use up your allotment by sunset. It's annoying."

"Oh." He sounded hurt.

"Drat it, Etienne. I'm sorry, it's this god-awful waiting. I was never very good at it."

"Don't I know it!" He grinned. "I once had to cut the electric to keep you home, to prevent what would have been a terrible automobile accident the night of your granddaughter, Jessica's, first dance recital."

I remembered my frustration that night, as I waited for my son to pick me up and drive me over to the auditorium. We planned to meet his wife there. It had been a miserable night of thunderstorms and blowing rain, dark as could be. As usual, Scott was timing it close to the wire and I became rammy, couldn't sit still. The ride to the auditorium took at least twenty minutes on a clear evening. When it was apparent we would be late, when it was ten minutes until show time, I decided to leave a note for Scott on the front door and drive over by myself, even though my night vision was poor and I was nervous about parking in the dark lot by myself. However, I just *had* to see Jessica; I could not miss her performance. My plans were foiled when the electricity suddenly went out. I had an electric garage door opener. Although it could be opened manually, it was one of the old-fashioned doors that weighed a ton; I didn't have the muscle to lift it. I started to walk over to the house next-door to ask my neighbor's husband for help with the door when Scott showed up, honking his car horn from a block away. We'd been late not only because Scott had not picked me up on time, but because we were further delayed by a terrible car accident on the way. A car had slipped on the slick, wet roadway and run head-on into one going in our direction. It appeared very serious. As it turned out, we were in plenty of time for Jessica's performance, because her dance number started after the intermission. What an absolute doll she had been up there on that stage in her orange and black tutu, dancing around with a little stuffed tiger to the tune of "Tiger Rag." She had, quite honestly, stolen the show.

"*You* cut the electric?"

"Yes ma'am, I sure did. It was a proud moment in my career.

I knew there was an accident scheduled down the road and wanted to avoid any possibility of your involvement. Carstairs agreed with me and allowed Scott to make all the green traffic lights on his way to pick you up."

"That was a Simple Intervention, wasn't it?"

"Rellie, you are quite the star pupil. It was indeed."

"Tell me, could that accident have happened to me if I'd not waited for Scott? How were the people?"

"Yes, it could have been you. The one woman was hospitalized with internal injuries, but survived; her husband and teenage daughter were not seriously injured; the driver of the car that hit them broke his leg."

"Oh, my. Thank you, Etienne." The more I got to know this soft-spoken man, the more I was thanking him. Perhaps my original assessment of him had been a bit too fierce. I should have realized sooner that anyone with eyes such as his and a voice so warm and tender could not be the ogre I'd imagined while wallowing in the depths of my wrath. I'd taken out my frustrations on the man and all he'd ever done was try to help me.

"It was a job and one of which I was very fond, Rellie. I lo …"

"I know." I smiled. I still couldn't let him say those words, because he would expect something back from me that I wasn't sure I wanted to give.

Conversations buzzed around us, as we found ourselves frozen in each other's eyes with nothing more to say. I must admit, this was so completely atypical of us both, that I was taken aback. It was not one of those comfortable little silences that occur between people who are at ease with one another. I couldn't help but remember something a teacher for the debating team in college once told me: "In an argument, state your case then wait, because the next person who speaks usually loses." I was afraid to speak, but knew not precisely what I could be losing if I did.

It wasn't a bell that saved us, but the sounds of a door slamming and running feet. We turned in the direction of the noise, waiting to see who would appear in the doorway. It was an extremely harried-looking Seymour, his hair was flying about his head in a very unkempt fashion, and he was gasping for breath.

Pen met him at the doorway and escorted him to the nearest seat. "Take it easy, Seymour. Catch your breath and tell us what happened." He sat in a chair beside Pen. Each of us brought a chair over to join them.

"I... I " He could still not speak.

"Take your time, Seymour. We're not going anywhere right now," Pen reassured him with a dazzling smile.

After several large gulps of air, Seymour leaped from his chair to face us. In a loud, proud voice he exclaimed: "It's been approved. Just now! The Complex Intervention is approved. The official approval should be coming over the fax as we speak ... as *I* speak ... whatever." He sagged into the empty chair beside him, as deflated as a balloon with a large hole in it.

Magically, Helga appeared at the door with a fax sheet in her hands. "This is for you, Penelope. Good news. Congrats." She handed the paper to Pen, turned and left us to our whooping and cheering. We all hugged. (Etienne held on to me longer than was necessary, but not long enough for my liking. That realization would require a lot of mulling when I had the free time for such a thing.)

"Read it to us, Pen," urged Mulligan.

"Yes, please hurry up and read it!" echoed Felicia.

"Okay, quiet down you guys and I'll do just that," Pen stood to face us. We calmed down as much as we could. "From the Complex Intervention Committee, copy to Heavenly Council, dated today just fifteen minutes ago ..."

Groaning audibly, Arlene urged, "Pen, get *on* with it, you're driving us nuts!" "Here! Here!" We agreed.

"Okay, I just wanted to give you the whole thing. Here goes: "In an unanimous agreement, the Committee hereby approves the proposed Complex Intervention by Guardian Angel Penelope in the interest of her charge, Marissa Butler. Furthermore, the Committee hereby grants Penelope permission to seek the assistance of the following Guardian Angels, upon their express agreement in writing, if so approached, to this Committee within the next twenty-four hours: Paul; Arlene; Sam; Mulligan; Laura; Felicia; and, Carstairs. Special permission will be accorded Guardian Angel Etienne, if he so chooses to participate, because Debarelle, his former charge and still-current responsibility, is the grandmother of the said Marissa Butler. It is further stipulated that Seymour, the former Guardian Angel in good standing of one Roger Kravin, is hereby given express permission to participate as a consultant to his former charge's behavior, but is expressly prohibited from direct involvement due to his recent resignation from Roger's case. If there are further additions requested for the Complex Intervention Team, these requests must be made in writing to the Committee within the next twelve hours. As usual, a full report for the Committee's review is expected upon the completion of the Intervention. Take care and good luck. We are proud of you and wish you blessed speed."

It was then I made up my mind. I would not be left behind to sit frustradedly, despondently, forlornly, or otherwise, on the sidelines in front of my EVR, to wait yet again. This time, I would participate; I would help my granddaughter.

"I'm going, too," I announced to a stunned group.

CHAPTER 23

By the time Otis arrived back at the Hellraisers' hideout, he remembered where he'd seen the scruffy old man who had been ascending the pig sty's steps as he was descending. He hurried to find Juan and was surprised to see Roger seated beside him.

"Hey, dude, you're famous, man!" he said to Roger. But Roger remained seated like a king and Otis had to stoop to shake his hand.

"Yeah, what's up?" asked Roger. "I heard you were missing. Trouble?"

"Nothing I couldn't handle." Otis sat on the other side of Juan, directing his words to him. "But now, yeah, there could be trouble, if I seen what I thought I seen just a bit ago."

"Tell,""directed Juan, as he rolled a cigarette paper full of marijuana.

"I spent a little time in the tank and …"

Juan scowled at Otis. "How many times I have to tell you, do your drinkin' at home, man. Right here with your friends. Stay outta trouble."

"I got other friends, *females*. And this one hot little piece was needin' some company. It's not good to drink alone, Juan. It was my gentlemanly duty to keep the dear girl company. It would not have been polite to refuse her hospitality." Otis grinned.

"Right. You're so full of shit, Otis, no wonder your eyes are brown. It's all that shit keeps your hair curly, too, ain't it?" Juan laughed. Roger laughed for the first time in days. It felt good; he loved this gang.

"Words, Otis, give me the words," Juan said, smoke sliding lazily from his nose.

"Yeah. So, anyways, this girl and me was havin' a party, a party for two, you know?"

"I know, get on with it." Juan was rapidly becoming impatient.

"She went to take a piss behind the garage. I just kept it warm while I waited. A cop came by and discovered I was not my normal, little, sober self. He took me with him. As the fine gentleman I am, I did not reveal there was a lady, whose condition was identical to my own, pissin' behind the garage. I expect to be properly rewarded for that gallantry very soon."

"Chivalry ain't dead, huh, Otis?" Mike asked, laughing with delight. He was still a virgin, but refused to admit it to any of the gang for fear they would think less of him. It was a condition he had been attempting to correct for several weeks, with no success.

"Yeah, kid. Anyways, I spent the night in the plush Police Suites." He shook his head as if to clear it. "Can't remember too much of it, except there was this dude in with me who wouldn't shut up, kept singing off-key about some amazing woman named Grace. Drove me to sleep."

"GET TO IT!" Juan's patience level had been breached.

"Okay, easy man. I'm impaired. I've got a headache bigger than my balls ... and that's BIG!" Otis laughed at his cleverness. All the others kept quiet. "Okay. So when I was leavin,' goin' down the outside stairs, I passed this old geezer todderin' up the steps. I looked at him; he looked at me. It was creepy. You know, I was sure I'd seen the dude before, just couldn't remember where, you know?"

All heads nodded.

"Anyways, I remembered where on my way back." He smiled.

"Big deal. Where?" Juan yawned.

Otis stood up to add import to his forthcoming announcement, his arms outspread as if in welcome. "He's the bum who was with that douche bag of a street bitch who died. He's the old fart Roger pushed out the way, the one whose nose was bleedin.'"

Juan, who had appeared to be bored during Otis's recitation, suddenly sat up as straight as a rod. His head jerked upward to look at Otis. "*That* guy was goin' *into* the police station *alone?* No one was draggin' him?"

"Yeah, man, I mean no. I jus' tol' you."

"He must know somethin,' man," Roger was nervous. "Why else would a scumball go *into* a police station?" He hopped up and started to pace frenetically up and down in front of Juan.

"Stop that! Lemme think," Juan jumped up. "How long ago did all of this happen?" he asked Otis.

"About forty-five minutes, max," was the reply.

"Okay, so all we have to do is go over there, hide somewheres, and wait for him to come out so we can beat the shit outta him. Easy. No prob. Cops are long-winded; he's probably still in there. Let's go. Rog, you stay here and wait till we get back, it won't do you no good getting' near the station or the old man."

In the blink of an eye, all the boys were gone, following Juan to the area of the police station. This left Roger alone to think. He was too antsy to sit still. He decided to take a walk and started down Delaware Avenue. What he saw along the side of the road gave him what he considered to be a most brilliant idea. In actuality, it became a major part of his undoing.

***

"Keep him in that cell and give him whatever he wants!" bellowed Sergeant Ramsey to his assistant, Larry.

"But, sir, he wants a bottle of bourbon," Larry said.

"Well, then, get him *two*," the sergeant grinned, "just keep him in there for the night."

Larry was a good assistant, but he was puzzled. Mister Robert was in the drunk tank and was fairly sober, not drunk enough to remain in there, that was certain. However, his sergeant was insisting they keep him and treat him like royalty. The man looked a bit ragged around all edges, if anyone wanted to know what he thought. They didn't, of course, but that didn't stop Larry from having opinions.

"Yes, sir. Right away, sir."

"Good. And Larry?"

"Yes, sir?"

"Maybe a little food would be advised. Find out what he likes and get it for him." Sergeant Ramsey handed him a twenty-dollar bill. "This is from petty cash."

Sergeant Ramsey breathed a sigh of relief. He glanced over in Mister Robert's direction. At least one of the players would be safe for the night and not out clogging up the works or getting himself killed. If he had to, he'd explain it to his Chief.

"Hurry back, we've got work to do."

"Yes, sir." Larry was definitely in a quandary. Usually the people you put into the cells were already drunk as skunks. This time, however, they had a reasonably sober man in a cell and were about to contribute to his inebriation by supplying him the booze with which to do it. This was a more interesting job than he had originally anticipated. Larry never realized, until too late, that his sergeant had been pulling his leg about the bourbon. By then, Mister Robert had finished one fifth and was singing loudly to the half-full second bottle.

✳✳✳

When the jubilant pandemonium calmed to a mere raucous level in the meeting room, we realized Helga was standing at the doorway, shouting. We could see her mouth moving; her eyebrows met in the middle of her forehead in a very serious frown. She looked like a fish out of water gasping for survival.

"Guys, Helga has something to say," I tried yelling, as I walked around the room, waving my arms. Eventually, it became quiet, as we directed our eyes and ears toward Helga.

"QUIET IN HERE!" Helga was caught hollering when we suddenly quieted down. "Ah, that's better. Thank you. You're carrying on enough to wake the dead." She laughed until she could hardly stand. Her humor was apparently infamous in these quarters. "Keep it down, folks. I guess I don't have to ask if the news is good. Just tone it down. Thanks." She pivoted on her left heel and headed down the hallway toward her office, head high and back stiffly erect.

Like a bunch of kids in school, we snickered behind our hands. "Was she in the military before coming here?" I asked. This started everyone literally rolling on the floor in fits of glee and uncontrolled laughter. Tears ran down their cheeks. I love a good laugh, but it helps to know what is so funny. "What's so damn funny?" I demanded, with my hands on my hips.

"Uh-oh. Better watch your language. Etienne, get her to watch her language around here," Felicia said, before once more erupting in laughter.

Etienne, struggling with his own humorous reaction, came to my rescue. I was no longer surprised that I'd begun looking in his direction whenever I needed assistance. He had not yet failed me; well, to amend that, he had not yet failed me here in Heaven. The jury, me, was still out on the Earth portion of his endeavors.

"Rellie, before Helga arrived in Heaven, she was a diva for the Russian Ballet Company. She revolutionized ballet as it was then known and later became a world-renowned choreographer. She was as light as the air and as delicate on her feet as a wisp of smoke. She floated across the stage as if blown by the merest suggestion of a gentle breeze, her feet never seeming to touch the floor." He was enthralled with memory.

"Good grief, she sure must have had a hell of a lot of repressed personality traits."

"Language, Rels, please."

"Right. A *ballerina?*" I burst into waves of joyful laughter, joining the rest of the group. "I'll bet she's in training to be reborn as Brunehilda the Second. That's what I'll bet."

Paul entered the room and walked to the front, giggling slightly before saying, "Okay, folks. We've got the approval, but there's still a lot of work to do, so let's get down to it."

We settled down and went over The Plan. A major part of this plan involved each participating guardian angel neutralizing his or her charge during the time needed for its' execution. Much discussion revolved around this topic, with the emphasis on the safety of each charge while unattended by their personal G.A., an extremely precarious situation at best. It was resolved as follows:

- Carstairs would arrange to have Scott (my son, Marissa's uncle) severely sprain his ankle and twist his shoulder, thereby putting him at the mercy of his wife, Justine, who would keep her eyes on him and force him to rest for the few hours required for the Complex Intervention.

- Sara (my daughter, Marissa's mother), explained Mulligan, would run out of gasoline on her way home, after leaving an antique shop far out in the country. She would be upset, but calmed thinking her husband, Alex, was at home by then to watch Rissa. She would forget to charge her cell phone.

- However, Alex would not be at home with Rissa, because Sam was going to cause the safe lock at his bank to malfunction while Alex was inside with his new clerk explaining the safe-deposit box system. The timer would assure them the time they needed for the Complex Intervention. Alex, dear lad, would be upset, but comforted believing Sara was at home with Rissa. He would leave his cell phone on his desk before entering the vault, as would his new employee.

- Laura had no great problems with Alex, Jr., except to make sure he remained at his computer camp. She'd "wing" it if any problems developed.
- As for Wren, Felicia would see to it that he won all the pizza he could eat in two hours. He would, of course, overindulge. His resultant gastrointestinal problems would keep him close to the porcelain bowl for hours.
- Arlene received great cooperation from Jamie's parents' G.A.s and reported that the entire family would be leaving for a week at the seashore, a special treat Jamie's father would announce on the spur-of-the-moment at dinner that very evening, much to everyone's delighted surprise, including his own. Reservations had been made and plans finalized with friends at the shore. They would not back out.
- Paul announced that Mister Robert was safe behind bars at the kind "invitation" of one Sergeant Ramsey of the Philadelphia Police.

That brought us to the star players: Rissa and Roger, with supporting roles from Juan, Otis, and Mike. This is where it all got tricky enough to worry me.

Paul continued: "With the extraneous people to this Complex Intervention temporarily sidelined, we come to Roger. Seymour?"

Seymour, who had been practicing shadow animals on the wall, had not been paying close attention to the plans, because he no longer had anything to do with Roger, not since his brilliant resignation earlier. What a relief it had been to purge himself of that looser. Everyone was aware how hard he had tried with Roger, but now and then you came upon a true incorrigible. Seymour had begun to teach that very morning, while he awaited his next guarding assignment. His mind was on the class, a bright bunch of N.A.s teetering on the brink of Acceptance.

"Seymour?" Paul repeated more forcefully.

"Huh? What, Paul? Sorry." He sat up straight, his hands folding into his lap as the shadow pterodactyl disappeared from the wall.

"We need your help with Roger."

"I'm no longer his GA, Paul. You all know I've resigned and been relieved in good standing from my duties in his behalf."

"Yes, we realize that, Seymour. But you also received special permission to consult with us on this Complex Intervention. We need your help in that capacity."

"What can I *do*? I know Roger's dark little soul down to its murky depths, but can that be of assistance?"

"It sure can, because you know how he thinks."

Interrupting, Seymour stressed, "Roger does *not* think. All he has ever done is to react. Thinking is a concept alien to his lexicon." He turned and tried a shadow sea turtle on the wall, with dismal success.

"Whatever." Paul showed signs of irritation. "This is no time for a discussion involving semantics, Seymour. We are here to help Rellie's granddaughter through a Complex Intervention. We must plan carefully."

As he shoved his hands into his pockets, Seymour said, "Yes, you're right. Sorry again. Tell me, what can I do?" Seymour was chagrined. He'd been so full of himself when he was relieved of Roger's case that he had allowed this relief to transcend all else.

"If you could screw him up, that'd be helpful."

"He's already screwed up, Paul."

"I mean, if we need you to suggest ways to trip him up, would you do it?"

"With a great deal of pleasure, yes, I would." He stood and took a theatrical bow. His friends clapped before he sat once more.

"Thank you, Seymour. Believe me, when we submit our report, you will get a good word for volunteering your expertise."

"Volunteering. Right. Thanks, Paul." Paul nodded and sat down, as Pen stood to take the stage.

"Now, we've got to watch what unfolds Down There. We know Juan is planning to steal a car and, along with Otis, Chun and Roger, make a visit to Marissa's house Monday afternoon, when she gets home from school. Are we ready?" she asked.

"Yes!" we all replied with great enthusiasm. After which I repeated, "And *I* am going along."

"No, Rellie. You and Etienne are to remain here. Etienne will remain with you, as he has no charge on Earth at this point. You are not trained for any type of Intervention work and, as such, cannot, must not, participate. You haven't even had one guardian angel class. I'm sorry, but that's the way it has to be." Pen was firm, her jaw was set.

I would not be deterred. "I *will* go. It is *my* granddaughter we're discussing here, not some stranger!" I said stubbornly, resisting the grand urge to stamp my foot. "I will go totally insane, if I have to wait behind with Etienne."

"Rellie, I promise not to drive you insane," Etienne said with a grin.

I looked at him. "You already have." To Pen, I said, "Damn it, you know what I mean. I *have* to go, Pen. Please! Maybe there's something I could do to help. Please think about it."

CHAPTER 24

What Roger considered his "brilliant idea" was inspired when he saw a dead pigeon lying in some litter at the curb beside the road. Roger kicked it with his foot. The little head flopped limply from side to side; its tiny neck had been broken. Roger continued walking for another block while considering his brainstorm and, in his convoluted thinking, he found the idea not only brilliant but foolproof. He retraced his steps, picked up the dead bird, and carried it back to the hideout before laying it on the ground by his feet. For five minutes he stared at it, just sat and stared, while savoring his idea. "Hot shit, but this is prime, man."

"What's that, Rog?" Mike's question startled Roger and caused him to jump.

"Nervous, Rog?" Mike knelt to look at the dead bird.

"No, I'm not nervous. You've no right sneakin' up on a guy. You could get shot for less, Mikey. What do ya think?" He poked the pigeon with a stick, which caused its head to loll over on its right side.

"I think it's dead, man. What you want with a dead sky rat for?"

"Michael, this here birdie is a gift for a dear friend of mine."

Mike stood up and walked over to an old stained box spring he'd lugged under the bridge during the past winter. He lay down on his back, arms beneath his head. "I think you're crazy, Rog. Just be nuts quietly. I'm gonna take a nap." He closed his eyes in dismissal of Roger.

A few minutes later, Juan and the boys came back, after having waited for the old man to come out of the police station.
They'd waited for two hours and didn't see him. They were pissed.

"Not to worry, he can't go far. We'll have fun with him later;
we know where to find him," Juan had told Mike, before leaving
with Otis and Chun for some Saturday night havoc. They'd left
him behind again, the assholes. Mike fell asleep with his angry
thoughts.

"I'll show you who's crazy, kid," Roger said to the now-sleep-
ing Mike. "No snot-nosed little creep who doesn't shave is gonna
tell me, Roger Kravin, I'm crazy. You don't know brilliance when
you see it. I'll show youse … all of youse!" Roger rolled the dead
bird into a filthy piece of newspaper, picked it up, hid it under a
hubcap, then rode off on the stolen bicycle.

Mike was dreaming he was at the seashore with a real family,
playing in the sand, body surfing on the warm waves, and eating
hotdogs with "the works" whenever he asked for one.

As Mike dreamed his favorite dream, Roger pedaled around
the city looking for Juan and the others. He thought of what he
would accomplish by this latest coup in his continued reign of
terror against the young girl and her family. He never realized his
actions were cementing their resolve for Rissa to testify against
him, when he was caught and brought to justice for Emma's death.
That he would eventually get caught was anathema to him. He
was enjoying his harassment of Marissa to the utmost. He'd already formulated plans to rape the girl once he got his chance,
and he would get it; he was convinced of his invincibility.

***

On Monday afternoon, as Roger carefully approached Rissa's
neighborhood, Sergeant Ramsey and his officers just as carefully
approached the location of the Hellraisers' hideout, as revealed by
Mister Robert. They spread out on both sides of the concrete bridge
abutment, guns drawn and back-ups in position. Mercifully, the

traffic on the bridge above helped muffle much of the noise the hard soles of their shiny black shoes made on the rubble beneath. Nevertheless, they continued slowly, with great caution, hoping to surprise the gang in repose, hoping Roger would be among them.

Sergeant Ramsey gave a signal to stop as he reached the side of the abutment. He moved forward, alone, as planned, following his gun around the corner at the same time he shouted, "Police, freeze! Don't anybody move! Hands where I can see them!" At this point, the other officers moved into position, ready to stop any who might try to run.

The eight officers froze in place, all aiming at a very surprised Mike, who was sitting upright on the soiled mattress, his eyes wide and his hands in the air, fingers spread. You had to look very closely to see he was still breathing.

"Relax," the sergeant told his officers. "Not you, son," he turned to Mike, who had lowered his arms. Once spoken to, he raised them higher than before. When he found he hadn't been shot, he found his voice. "I dint do anything, officer. What's the matter? I was jus' takin' a nap. No law against that, is there?"

Sergeant Ramsey holstered his gun and walked over to Mike. "Stand up." Mike stood. "What's your name, boy?" Mike told him. "Okay, Mike. Where are the rest of them?"

"Rest o' what?"

"Let's do this nice and easy, shall we? You want to get back to your nap and we have work to do."

"I doan know what you're talkin' about, sir." Juan had told them, if you have to talk to a cop, always call him a nice, polite "sir;" they love that shit. And smile like you was a little choir boy. Mike had never seen a choir boy smile or do anything else; hell, he'd never gotten that close to a church, but he scrunched his mouth into what he felt was an appropriate little sincere-looking smile.

"How old are you, Mike?"

"Almost seventeen." he lied.

"Un, huh. Almost in about three years, right?"

Mike said nothing, just stood there, suddenly having to pee a river.

The sergeant had the other officers come over and stand in front of Mike. "Wait here while Mike and I have a little chat, then we'll go over to the station. Do you want to talk with me here, Mike, or would you like to go on over to the police station with us? It's up to you, but you have to decide right now. I'm not farting around with this any longer."

"Okay, here. Let's talk here. Who you lookin' for?" Mike sighed. His bladder was aching.

"I'm looking for Roger Kravin. When was the last time you saw him?"

Mike was still smarting from Juan, Otis, and Chun leaving him behind again. They never let him have any fun. Roger was never very nice to him neither, treating him like a little pain in the ass kid. He'd show them all. "Roger was here before I fell asleep."

"What time was that?"

"I don't know. Maybe an hour ago. I don't know." If he didn't pee soon, he'd burst. The best he could do now was to talk fast, tell 'em anything they wanted to know. And that is precisely what he did: the dead bird, Juan and the boys planning to steal a car, Roger stalking that girl.

"Get out of here, Mike. There's still time for you to make something of yourself," the sergeant said kindly.

He was having chills, he had to go so bad. "Ummm," he said.

"Think about what I said," the sergeant said, before he and the others climbed the embankment out from under the bridge.

It was too late; Mike had wet his pants just like a baby. He was so ashamed, he lay down on the mattress and, also like a baby, cried out his frustration, embarrassment, and growing fear that Juan would find out who had ratted. Juan found out everything.

***

While Sergeant Ramsey was notifying the police local to Marissa's school and home, the Complex Intervention Team, as they were referring to themselves, were making concessions to me.

"Okay," Pen said. "Let's put this to a vote. Who wants Rellie to accompany us *strictly as an observer*," she emphasized, with a stern look in my direction. I smiled and bit my lower lip in nervous anticipation. "Etienne, you will be required to go along with her to watch her, if it is so agreed. Is this acceptable to you?" He nodded his accent. "Okay, with a show of hands, who thinks Rellie should go with us to observe *only*?"

It was unanimous; I was going along! My heart sang. I was sure I'd figure a way to help my Rissa if necessary, but I didn't share *that* with the group.

"No," Etienne appeared at my side, gently taking my right hand in both of his and looking into my eyes. "No you won't."

"Shit. This has got to stop. I can't have you reading my mind all the time." I withdrew my hand.

"I'm not reading your mind. I just *know* you, and you were thinking you'd get involved somehow. Am I right?"

"Yes. But, if ..."

"I'll keep you here, Rellie. By Jove, I will! Are you going to behave?"

"I'm not a child, Etienne. Yes, of course, I'll behave, but you can't blame me for wanting to personally strangle Roger Kravin!"

"No, but we have a bit more finesse here in Heaven, Rellie. Let the G.A.s do their job."

I turned from Etienne's eyes with great difficulty and said to the roomful of people, "Thank you. I won't let you down. I realize you are the experts in this sort of thing and defer to your expertise. I'm just so worried. Let's hurry, please."

It was decided that we would all wear the stereotypical white Flowing Robe on Monday afternoon, as well as special-issue temporary wings because, as Mulligan was so wise to point out, "People are quite *dim* in general, Roger in particular. We must look the part according to his little mind." Hence, the robes and wings. I must admit, I looked kind of cute in mine; Etienne was ravishingly handsome in his.

We would soon be on our way.

CHAPTER 25

When Officer Janis Monroe heard the call to "check the well-being" at Rissa's house, she was less than a mile away. "I've got it, Hank," she radioed the dispatcher. Because of recent activity at that house, all of the local officers were aware of the situation. Janis thought she might need back-up, but decided to check it out first. She turned left and headed toward Marissa's house.

Moments earlier, Rissa had stepped from the school bus, which now stopped directly across from her house. The driver had been advised to watch until she entered the front door and shut it behind her. The bus was equipped with a cellular telephone in the event of a problem.

The driver, retired gym teacher, Manny Brophy, idled the bus and returned Marissa's wave as she entered her house, arms laden with books for her latest history project. Manny had not noticed Rissa step over a box that sat on her front door step. He tooted the horn, before moving along to complete his run; there were still ten students in his bus who were anxious to get home. None of the students complained about the stop at Marissa's house. They knew the story, although they felt their own parents had become excessively protective because of it. They were anxious for the jerk to be caught and locked up, so their lives could return to the way they'd been before "that awful thing happened to the little Butler girl."

As mentioned, Manny had not seen Rissa step over the package on the front step. He would later state, unequivocally, that he had watched Marissa open her front door, wave the "all's well" signal, then close the door behind her, before he drove off to finish his job for the afternoon.

When she saw the package by the door, Rissa's arms were so full of study materials and books that she couldn't pick it up as she inserted the key into the door. "Oh, great! A present for me. The UPS man must have left it. I wonder what it is?" she thought as she opened the door and waved at the bus driver. After placing her books and notebooks on the table in the entry hall, she reopened the front door, quickly looked both ways, and scooped the package inside, immediately locking the door securely behind her. She put the box on the table beside her books and headed for the kitchen to get a snack. She decided to let the package wait a while to heighten the anticipation.

Rissa spread a bagel with cream cheese, placed it on the plate she had removed from the cabinet, and was pouring some cold milk into her favorite mug, when the doorbell rang. Normally, she would not have hesitated to rush to the door and open it to see who was there. Now, however, she approached the door cautiously, rising on her toes to peek into the peep hole her father had installed after Roger began his harassment. "Who's there?" she called.

"Officer Monroe, Janis Monroe. Go over to the window and I'll show you my credentials."

"Okay." Rissa moved toward the front window in the living room. Once satisfied with what she saw, she opened the door for Janis. "Is something wrong?"

Officer Monroe looked around. "I don't think so. You Marissa?" The girl was obviously nervous, poor thing. Janis knew from the reports that this girl had been through a lot recently. "We got a call from a Sergeant Ramsey downtown in Philadelphia. He asked us to check on you; he wasn't able to reach either of your parents. He thinks that boy, Roger, could be headed this way again. The sergeant asked us to make sure all was secure and you were safely in from school."

"Yeah. You know it's like I'm the one in jail and Roger's free. It's not fair, is it?" Rissa shook her head sadly. "Sometimes, I think it's not worth it, but then I remember that poor old lady. She died."

Janis patted Rissa gently on her shoulder. "I know, honey. But you should be very proud of yourself. Believe me, you're doing the right thing by testifying. It seems like forever right now, but we'll get him. I promise. It won't be much longer." She wasn't at all sure about that, but the kid was down. "Let me take a quick look through, and then I'll be on my way. Anyone else here?"

"Just my brother, Wren."

"Where's he?"

"Upstairs in the bathroom throwing up. He won all the pizza he could eat at the Pizza Spot after school and made a pig out of himself. Now all he can do is throw up. What a jerk. *Brothers.*" Rissa wrinkled her nose in mock disgust.

Janis chuckled as she began her search of the house. All appeared to be secure and in order. "Lock up behind me. I won't leave until I hear the locks click."

Marissa watched as Janis got into the patrol car and drove down the street, turning right at the corner. As she turned, she saw the package on the hall table. She picked it up and took it into the kitchen with her.

Roger was across the street, where he sat on the curb between a dented red Astro van and a dirty white Roto Rooter truck. He had the bicycle on the ground beside him and was busy pretending to fix the tire, in case someone started to wonder what he was doing there. He saw the school bus arrive and watched as Rissa stepped over the package, returning within seconds to take it inside with her. He waited in eager delight for the squeal of outrage he was sure would follow, but it didn't happen. Instead, he watched in dismay as a cop—a *broad*, big laugh!—went inside the house. She wasn't in there very long before she drove away, in no apparent hurry. No other cops showed up. He breathed a sigh of relief. The longer he waited for Marissa to open the package, the more nervous he became. He didn't believe she could open it and not react. He couldn't hang there too much longer, but he sure wanted to be around for the reaction he was convinced would be stupendous. He felt so damn clever; he had to see this with his own eyes. He'd wait five more minutes, then he'd better move on. He gave the front bike wheel a spin, as he pictured her opening the box while wondering who'd sent her a present. He imagined how she'd read the note, his work of art: "This is yu prity ladee if yu sing." She'd be puzzled and increasingly apprehensive, but her curiosity would get the better of her. She'd peel back the newspaper to reveal the dead pigeon lying there, its neck broken and staring glassily up at her from sightless eyes, its body already starting to decompose and smell.

He did not have long to wait until he heard a loud scream from inside the house. Although the windows were opened only two inches, because of the newly installed safety locks, the scream came through loud and clear. He hadn't realized how aroused he'd become and ejaculated as the third scream penetrated the air. He was stunned by his reaction and froze for a moment, before jumping onto the bicycle and riding hell-bent for the wooded area behind the house, his vantage point.

Meanwhile, Juan, Otis, and Chun drove toward Rissa's house, following the directions Roger had given them. When they left, Mike was asleep, which was good, Juan thought, because they didn't want the little punk along anyhow. They had found a brand new red Celica parked on Fifth Street near Catherine Street with the keys in it.

"It's a sign, man," Chun said. "If they's left the keys, they's meaning for us to have it."

It was unanimous; the Celica was theirs. Juan drove it around the corner and stopped, while Otis removed the license plate, replacing it with one they had taken earlier from a four-year-old blue Hyundai parked at the curb.

They were quickly on their way and had not noticed the little girl as she watched their antics from the window of her row home on Catherine Street. She immediately went in to her baby brother's room, where her mother was nursing him. "Some bad boys just took the license plate off our car. Why would they do that, Mommy?"

∗∗∗

It was strange being back on Earth, but there was no time to think about it, there was work to be done. Etienne stayed close to me the entire way, a floaty sort of journey that seemed to take no more than a few seconds. We had all stood on a high, white platform over on the extreme west side of Heaven. We stood in a circle, facing outward, holding hands. A soft mist enveloped us and I felt a gentle floating sensation as I clutched Etienne's hand in my right and Mulligan's in my left. In what seemed like seconds, we arrived in Rissa's backyard. I must admit there were tears in my eyes, as I recalled the happy picnics and play times I'd enjoyed with my grandchildren in that yard.

"Are you okay?" ever-diligent Etienne asked softly.

"Yes, I'll be just fine. Thank you."

Before letting go, he squeezed my hand. "Remember, Rellie, we are here to observe, *not* to participate. We must let the others do their job."

"I know, I know." I was watching the others mill about, when a scream sliced the air, quickly followed by two more. Marissa!

Before I had time to run toward the house, Pen shouted, "Etienne, hold her right here! The Intervention is beginning; all players are in position, now it unfolds. Take her under those trees at the back of the property and *keep her there!*" Pen was off and running.

From our vantage point beneath the trees, we watched as everyone bustled about for the Complex Intervention. It was done with wonderful precision. I was a nervous wreck. This was almost worse than watching it on my EVR, because I was here and still couldn't do a thing to help. I gazed around and saw movement in the bushes behind Etienne. "Etienne," I whispered.

"You don't have to whisper, Rellie. No one but I can hear you."

I continued to whisper. "I'm not at all sure about that. There's someone behind you in those bushes." I pointed.

"Really? Or are you trying to trick me so you can go running to the house?"

The thought had crossed my mind. He knew me well. "No!" I practically hissed. "Please check it out; it could be Roger."

Etienne nonchalantly strolled over to the bushes, his hands on his hips, to look around. It didn't take him long before he called to me. "It's Roger, all right. Keep an eye on him. I'll go tell Pen. Don't try to do anything, Rellie. If he leaves, just notice which way he goes. Don't follow him."

"Okay." I stood guard and wished quite fervently that I knew how to cause him great distress. I concentrated on boils, picturing him covered from head to toe with suppurating boils. I blinked. His skin remained boil free.

I was so involved in my thoughts, it took me a moment to realize that Roger was walking directly toward me. Well, not toward *me* actually, but toward Marissa, who had chosen that moment to come out of her back door to toss a dead pigeon onto the lawn. She is a wonderful child, but this seemed strange behavior. In a purely reflexive reaction, I ran toward her across the soft, green lawn and shouted with all of my strength: "Rissa! GET BACK INSIDE NOW, QUICKLY! LOCK THE DOOR!"

At that moment, several things happened at once. The guardian angels came rushing from all directions into the back yard, which caused Roger to stop in his tracks. His mouth fell open and his eyes became as large as saucers in his suddenly pale face. He looked as if all the blood had drained from his body. The angels had revealed themselves to him.

Marissa gasped as she saw Roger, turned and ran directly into the house. She slammed the door shut, locked it, and leaned against it, her hand to her heart. "Grams?" her voice was incredulous. "Grams, was that you? I thought I saw you for a split second and I heard your voice! Oh, Grams, you saved me!" She smiled.

Etienne was beside me in a tick. "I thought I specifically told you to stay put, stay out of it."

"But, I ..."

"WOW! Are we glad you didn't! You're a marvel, Rellie. I had no idea you had so much energy to project. You saved your grand-daughter!" He hugged me.

"How was I able to do it?" I felt weak.

"Love."

We stood closely together and watched as the guardian an-gels, all holding hands, moved toward Roger at a slow but steady pace. The angels had revealed themselves only to Roger, so what Marissa saw from the safety of her kitchen window seemed noth-ing less than miraculous (which it was, of course).

Roger stood, as if frozen, his mouth hung open and drool ran down his chin onto his neck, only to nestle in a soggy puddle inside the dirty collar of his green T-shirt. As the angels moved ever closer, he found his feet and his voice at the same moment. He began running in circles, flailing his arms wildly. "Angels! An army of angels! Fuckin'-a, the girl's got angels after me. This ain't fair! Where the hell'd they come from? *Angels*? Help me!"

When the angels were almost upon him, smiles fixed upon their faces, they began to chant: "Roger Kravin, we are going to get you. There's no where to hide, no where to run. You killed Emma. You can't get away. No where to hide, no where to run. Roger Kravin, we are going to get you. There's no where to hide, no where to run. You killed Emma. You can't get away. No where to hide, no where to run." Over and over, they chanted, as they ever so slowly and steadily approached Roger.

"Rog, where are you?" Juan shouted, as he pulled the Celica up to the curb at the front of the house. Like the idiot he was, he even tooted the horn.

"HELP! HELP!" Roger screeched, as he broke and ran for the car, Juan, and sanity. "HELP! There's a bunch of damn frickin' angels after me!" He wind-milled his arms in an attempt to remain on his feet as he frantically ran.

Otis opened the rear door of the Celica and Roger barreled in. "There's angels, man! See them?" He pointed to the angels who had surrounded the car, bending to look in at all of the windows, and still chanting their lament.

"Let's get outta here, man! They're after me, Juan. Otis? Chun? No! They're lookin' at me, they're all around the damn car!" He cringed. He screamed. He twitched.

"Shit, man. You're crazy. Angels? There's no such thing, dude. Sit still, you'll ruin the upholstery." Juan turned to look at Roger, who was plainly crazed. "Second thought, Chun, escort Roger from the vehicle, if you will. Looney tunes we don't need. When you sober up, or dry out, or crash, or whatever you need to do, then we'll talk. Lie low and snap out of it, Rog. Maybe all you need is a good crap."

"No, no, no, no … Don't make me get out. They're waitin' for me. *Look!* See them? They've surrounded the frickin' car, for chrissake. I'm tellin' you, they're mean lookin' angels, man. Drive away, hurry." Roger was shaking uncontrollably, his eyes had a fevered glaze. He reached for Juan.

"Get the crazy bastard outta this car *now!*" Juan screamed.

Chun and Otis had a struggle, but managed to push and pull a still-raving Roger from the car. After not so gently depositing him at the curb directly at the feet of the angels, Juan sped away, leaving Roger to his fate.

Marissa had called 9-1-1, and the police appeared several minutes later to find a babbling Roger more than a little eager to get into one of the three police cars that had pulled up at the curb.

"Hurry up! Take me with you, get me away from these angels, man. Hurry up, just shut them up, will you? Tell them to go away," he pleaded to the astonished officers. "Leave me alone!" he shouted to what looked to the police to be thin air.

"No, Roger Kravin, we've got you now. There's no where to hide, no where to run. You killed Emma. You can't get away. No where to hide, no where to run."

"NO! NO!" he was sobbing now, his hands over his ears. The angels wouldn't shut up. "Go away, please go away!" he continued to plead.

As the police car drove away with Roger, his screaming and sobbing could be heard until they turned the corner at the far end of the street.

✳✳✳

The angels stood watching until the car was out of sight.

"He said 'please,'" Seymour said. "Isn't that something? I never heard him say that before." He grinned. "Too late, though."

At which point, there was much joyous jumping around, back patting, and cheering. It was wonderful. My Rissa was safe, thanks to this terrific group of guardian angels, my friends. I was so moved, I threw my arms around Etienne and kissed him full on his mouth. The look of surprise on his face was priceless. "Etienne, you are truly a treasure," I said. "Thank you for being, well, *you*." I kissed him again.

His arms had tightened around me. He showed no intention of letting me go. He tilted his head back so he could look into my eyes. "I love you, Debarelle."

"I know," I said. "I lo … know."

"Our work is finished here," Pen announced. "Take hands, it's time to go back." And so we did.

CHAPTER 26

Q ur return was triumphant. Saint Peter had the Heavenly chorus and marching band waiting for us at the platform. The Intervention Committee was assembled and smiling. Our friends were there with Thelma and Ian at the head of the receiving line, when we disembarked the platform.

One of the more touching moments occurred when Emma, accompanied by her Jimmy, walked over to the group, her face awash with ecstasy. "Thank you, everyone!" she exclaimed. "You were wonderful." Great whoops of happiness resounded throughout Heaven.

It was amid all of this elation that tragedy struck. Wilbur once again ran breathlessly up to Etienne. "She's in labor, Etienne, your new mother just went into labor! It's her second. You'll have an older brother, so it wont take her too long. You have to get to the Reborning Platform right away!" Wilbur hopped up and down in a nervous little jig. "This time, Etienne, it's no mistake. You must come with me *now!*"

"No, Wilbur, I can't, not *now!*" He pleaded. He turned those velvety eyes on me.

"You must, you know the rules. You accepted them when you agreed to be reborn. Now's the time." Wilbur tried to take hold of Etienne's arm, but he jerked it away.

"I just can't. Not *now*. Wilbur, buy me some time. A day, even. Could you manage that?"

"Yes, I can. We can do a false labor for a day, and have her sent home. But only one day, Etienne. Be there on the Reborning Platform by noon tomorrow, not a jot later."

"I'll be there," Etienne assured him. "Thanks, Wilbur."

That's when I knew I loved Etienne. Typically, when you think you've lost or are losing someone, that's when you realize how important they are to you. Perversity doesn't seem to stop just because you're in Heaven. There was suddenly so much I wanted to say to Etienne, and now he was going to leave, go away for ever so long! Maybe our new schedules would never coincide again.

"Etienne! Could I come, too?"

This surprised the hell, er, *heck* out of Etienne. "Why, Rellie?" The bugger wasn't giving an inch, not even in his distress.

"Because I want to," I equivocated.

"Why would you want to?" Rascal.

"Because I want to know you better. Because I enjoy your company. Because ..." I wound down.

"I love you, Rellie."

Okay. "I love you, too, Etienne." There. I'd said it. Furthermore, I meant it with all my heart and soul.

With that, he grabbed my hand and we ran for the Reborning Schedules. We spent hours pouring over them, trying to find a family for me, a place near where he would be living. When I wasn't looking at potential parents, I reviewed Etienne's Guardian Angel report on me. He'd done a superb job in spite of me. I quickly signed my approval on the bottom line.

Thelma the Romantic and Ian the Tender, in our behalf, went to the Reborning Committee and managed to push through a rush order.

"How'd you do it?" I asked.

"Don't worry about it, Rellie," Ian smiled. "We made them an offer they couldn't refuse."

"I saw that movie, Ian, it didn't end too well. Thelma, what gives? You two aren't in any trouble, are you?"

Thelma hugged me and said they were not in trouble. It was, actually, just the opposite. She was between guardian gigs and Ian had just decided he wanted to be a G.A. Their 'deal' tied in with those facts.

"What? But, how …"

They were saved further explanation by the blaring of the horn. Etienne and I had to go. Our thanks, hugs, and kisses were shared quickly. I couldn't help thinking both Thelma and Ian looked like the proverbial cat that ate the canary; I could almost see feathers on their lips, they looked so content with themselves.

After an all-nighter crash course, a course that normally can take as much as a week, I was deemed reborn material. I was ready. By 11:55 the next morning, exhausted, we ran to the Reborning Platform, handed in our tickets, and stood in position, side by side but not touching.

As with the Intervention, a lovely, warm, soft mist began to envelop us. I immediately panicked. What if this didn't work? What if I never saw him again? I'd not always been nice to him, while he had been nothing less than wonderful to me. Who gave a shit … a damn … a *darn* … if he couldn't tell his right from his left? I loved him.

"Etienne!" I called. The mist was thickening. I could see only his shape, his tall form. His wonderful features were blurred, and those fabulous eyes were hidden in the mist. "Etienne!"

"Rellie! It's okay. We'll be together."

"I love you, Etienne!"

"I know," he said, before the mist took us.

EPILOGUE

Juan, Otis, and Chun were killed later the same evening that Roger was taken into custody, when the stolen Celica was spotted by the police. Rather than submit to arrest, Juan tried to outrun the cops. A light spring rain had begun to fall, wetting the leaves that had been blown onto the highway by the strong wind that had accompanied the storm. Lightening flashed, tearing through the darkened sky as thunder rolled around the pursuers and the pursued. A high-speed sharp turn on the slippery leaves resulted in the car rolling over twice before landing, with a resounding crash, on its roof, crushing the three occupants inside. Luckily, no other vehicles were involved.

✻✻✻

Young Mike tried to continue the bump-and-grab operation on his own around Independence Mall. A month after his friends' deaths, he made the mistake of bumping and grabbing the wallet of a former FBI agent on vacation, who grabbed him and personally escorted him to the police station. Mike was sent to a juvenile home and later, with the help of Sergeant Ramsey, to the foster home of the Reverend and Mrs. Walters who, it so happened, owned a summer home at the seashore. It was with this family, who had four other foster children, that he played in the sand, body surfed on the warm waves, and ate hotdogs with 'the works,' maybe not whenever he asked for one, but often enough to be wonderful. Under the loving and often boisterous guidance of this family, Mike grew and healed. He later became a social worker and worked with inner city kids.

With the deaths of its strong leadership, the Hellraisers gang disbanded, as each member slowly drifted over to other gangs. They continue to wreak havoc in the streets of Philadelphia.

Flowers continue to bloom near the spot where Mister Robert lovingly buried Emma's little gold ring with the small diamond chip. Mister Robert continues to go to the corner of Sixth and Chestnut Streets every day around noon and remembers the lovely lady he met there. He misses her less as the days go by, but the memory of his friend never dims. He drinks as much, perhaps more, when he finds the money. He continues to hold close his dream of meeting his grandson. This will not happen on Earth.

Roger Kravin was placed in a psychiatric hospital and will never be considered well enough to stand trial for Emma's murder or the harassment of Marissa. He never rests completely and is continually heard screaming to be rescued from "the angels." Behind his back, he is often referred to as 'Ravin' Kravin.'

Marissa once more became the happy, carefree young girl she had been prior to her class trip to Independence Mall. When her friends suggested a trip to the same area the following summer, she went, thus dispelling her 'ghosts.' For the rest of her life, she was firm in the belief that her Grams was the one who had loved her so much that she had come from Heaven to help her.

Her brother, Wren, would never again eat pizza.

***

The two women had been friends since high school, from which they had been graduated ten years. Their husbands were golfing buddies, having met through their wives who also played golf. The couples lived on the same street, five houses apart. The houses in the comfortable middle-class development were alike in design. It was through the creative use of paint and plantings that each owner individualized their property. Each couple had one child, a son of three years. Each woman was expecting her second child. For one of the women, the second child would be her final child; for the other, a third child would be born two years later. Both marriages were solid and would remain so throughout their lives. Their current residence would be the only home their children would know as they grew. Both couples would eventually retire to North Carolina.

The two women gave birth on the same day, within thirty minutes of each other. There was a son for one and a daughter for the other. Everyone agreed that both babies were beautiful. Once they were up and about, the women met for a visit to introduce the babies to each other, while their two older children played in the sandbox in the fenced backyard.

The mothers watched their offspring closely as they sat in the shade of the maple trees. The babies had been placed side by side in a well-padded Pack 'N Play® Playard near their mothers. After a few moments, one mother remarked: "My goodness! Isn't that the oddest thing? Our babies have the same birthmark. Look!"

Upon closer investigation, it was proven true. Each baby had what appeared to be a small mushroom-shaped birthmark on its arm near the elbow.

"For Heaven's sake!" exclaimed the other mother. "That must mean they'll be special friends."

The women laughed delightedly and continued their pleasant chat, content in each other's company.

The baby girl and the baby boy lay, side by side, their little arms flailing about, little fists swinging, and their strong, tiny legs beating a rhythm in the warm air. Each was aware of the other, which made both of them feel very good. As they wiggled about, their heads turned toward each other, their little eyes focused intently on the other's face. Both became exceedingly still. The baby girl gurgled contentedly; the baby boy smiled his first smile.

"We did it!" cooed the little girl.

"Thank Heaven," the little boy babbled around a wonderful bubble on his lips.

***

In Heaven, Thelma and Ian stood, side by side, in front of her Earth Views Receiver. "It'll be okay now. I'll watch over him. I'm glad we agreed to this and were able to rush your courses," Thelma said.

"Yes, me, too. I'll take care of her," Ian replied, as he took Thelma's hand in his. "All is as it should be."

They smiled joyously.

***

The wonderful moment between the babies passed as quickly as it had come. Thus, began the unfolding of time—hours, days, and years of it—time that would erase their memories of their other time. New joys and challenges would occupy them. They would be the best of friends their entire lives, and to this friendship, when they became young adults, they would add love. Their lives together would not always be easy, but they would forever be filled with love; and, they had two loving guardian angels to watch over them.

Thank Heaven!

ABOUT THE AUTHOR

Before devoting much of her free time to writing, Renée Plank Savacool worked for many years as a textbook editor at a college in suburban Philadelphia. Previous to that time, she was both the editorial/marketing assistant for a publisher of young adult non-fiction as well as the managing editor of a publishing company that specialized in the preservation of individual life stories. Renée is also a freelance journalist; her articles and stories have appeared in local newspapers and national magazines. She is married and lives in Pennsylvania.

The
Heaven
Handbook

Contents

Welcome to Heaven

Heaven is a place of extraordinary and special natural beauty as well as rich and vibrant heritage. Heaven, literally, is the place of dreams come true.

Introduction

Heaven. Few people have not, at some point in their lives, heard of it. Many have wondered about it. There are many preconceptions about Heaven.

Heaven has been both well advertised and misrepresented on Earth. This handbook, combined with your own observations and experiences, will serve to acclimate you properly to Heaven as it is today.

Many changes have occurred in Heaven, the most recent being the addition of climate-control panels into each private residence. Guardian Angel School enrollment has grown 34 percent over the past two centuries.

The word *heaven* evokes various images in the minds of living persons. Common to the majority of these images is that Heaven is a place of peace and joy, where physical pain does not exist. This is true, however, as you will find, Heaven is much, much more. Life in Heaven is not a stagnant existence nor is it a boring one. Heaven is a bustling, busy place and all residents are required to participate.

Climate

As one would expect of a perfect place, Heaven is blessed with a benign climate; it is neither too warm nor too cool. It does not rain in main Heaven. For those of you who desire a bit of variety in your weather, you are welcome to visit special sections created for your pleasure, such as: Snow Mountain; Windy Valley; Sunbeam Seashore; Gasping Gulch; Muddy Mesa; Thunder Plateau; Twister Prairie; Shivering Trails; and Hurricane Point; to name a few.

Geography

The Heavenly topography is basically level with millions of lakes, streams, rivers, oceans, and some gently rolling hills. Those who wish variety can always visit the special sections, some of which are listed above. (For a more detailed list, please submit a written request in your nearest Request Box.)

Time

Time has been adjusted to Earth-type conceptions in order to ease your existence in Heaven. Therefore, one will find a 24-hour day: daylight and nighttime hours are each of twelve hours' duration. This does not vary by even one minute. This arrangement has proven satisfactory and is most equitable to both our "day people" and our "night people."

Cultural Environment

Heavenly history has always been such that it allows all ethnic groups equal access. It should be noted that every individual on Earth is encouraged to come to Heaven; and equal opportunities are afforded on Earth to all who so desire.

We in Heaven are proud to tell you that every race is well represented here. Fast upon this fact, one must also point out that all races live happily together in Heaven, unlike on Earth. Everyone is equal here in all respects.

Language

The common language of Heaven is Heavenese, a wonderful blend of all spoken language. Whatever a resident's native tongue, upon arrival, he/she immediately has the ability to understand and communicate with everyone in Heaven.

Transportation

Getting to Heaven

While some persons plan their trip with great forethought and detail, most residents arrive without prior arrangements. This condition generally results in a bit of surprise, which can lead to both anger and frustration in varying degrees. Heaven is well equipped to deal with these temporary complaints. After a few moments with friends and loved ones at the Main Gate Reception area, most persons are acclimated quickly. Private counselors are on 24-hour call to help any who wish to seek assistance.

Getting Around in Heaven—Our Road System

A road map is enclosed in the back pocket of your handbook along with a pullout map of the Main Reception area at the center of the handbook.

Roads are laid out in an easily comprehended grid pattern similar to those in center-city Philadelphia, Pennsylvania, on Earth. Numbered streets in Heaven run north-to-south; named streets run east-to-west. It is a tried and true pattern.

Road Assistance Kiosks

These are situated every two miles in a park area in the center of the road to aid travelers. (*Note:* Traffic jams are non-existent, however, we must caution you there is ALWAYS an increase of traffic in the Convention/Auditorium area whenever there is a

Guardian Angel [G.A.] Convention or when St. Peter is scheduled to speak at special seminars and/or meetings. Please allow extra time to arrive and be seated.)

Modes of Transportation

Foot travel comprises approximately 90 percent of all Heavenly travel. Our system of gliding walkways and stationary footpaths is immense, well maintained, and growing daily. Foot travelers have access to all sections of Heaven.

Mini-gliders are single-seated personal hovercrafts and are provided to each resident. Most often, these are utilized when visiting our special sections (see climate and geography headings), such as Snow Mountain or Windy Valley, or for arriving at rock concert areas.

Skyway Cabs are commercial gliders similar to the personal miniglider and can transport up to two hundred travelers at a time. There are Skyway Cab depots strategically located throughout Heaven and extremely convenient scheduling is offered. (*Note:* Schedules are available through your Request Box.)

Accommodations

Cloudlettes

No matter what type of housing you were accustomed to on Earth, your every need has been anticipated in your new heavenly home. One of the first orders of business upon your arrival is to settle you into your private cloudlette dwelling. After you have been processed through the Main Gate and been greeted by family, friends, and well-wishers, you will be escorted to your new residence. Every cloudlette is the same and consists of a time-honored floor plan. All amenities are available to you from the moment you move in. There are, of course, no rent, mortgage, tax, or utility payments required. This residence is permanent as long as you reside in Heaven, which could be forever.

Earth Views Receiver (EVR)

Every individual is issued an EVR (Earth Views Receiver). This device is similar to Earth television yet goes far beyond that elementary technology. We realize how important those left behind are to our residents, especially to our new arrivals. It is with this in mind that Heaven provides not only the standard heavenly channels (similar to cable television, but free), but also allows each individual to select special personalized channels. These special channels allow the viewer to watch different people on Earth as they live their lives on a day-to-day basis. Viewers of these channels are cautioned prior to each transmission, because it is possible for the viewing matter to occasionally alarm some viewers.

Telephone

Every person is issued a home phone in the color of his/her choice. Cell phones are part of the standard communications package. There is no charge and all calls to all heavenly areas are free. Service is excellent and breaks in communication are not possible.

Request Boxes

Easily identified, these pastel pink, blue, and yellow boxes are similar to American mailboxes. Request Boxes are located within four cloudlettes of every residence. Anything you want can be requested, in writing, by using a 3 x 5 card (provided at no charge in boxes of 1,000) and dropping it into the box nearest your cloudlette. Be sure to indicate your cloudlette number and your name. Most requests are fulfilled within two hours, however, it is advisable to allow a maximum of one heavenly day for fulfillment of your request. (Online requests are not as efficient, and two heavenly days should be allowed if you use this form of request.)

Dining

Eating establishments in Heaven offer a wide range of food from haute cuisine to rapid food. Heavenly fare suits every dining mood. No reservations are necessary at any of our fine restaurants. (*Note:* Eating is optional in Heaven. We are, however, aware that many people enjoy both the process and the sociability involved, hence, it is provided. Food and drink are available in private cloudlettes as well as in eateries of every description and size. A resident can eat or drink whatever he/she desires, as much and as often as desired, and need not worry about gaining weight, becoming inebriated, or being in any way uncomfortable. After all, this is Heaven.)

Entertainment/Cultural Facilities

Heaven is the hub of culture and entertainment. It is here you can meet writers, philosophers, discus throwers, actors, sculptors and artists, baseball players, polo players, and so on, if they are in residence and have not chosen reborning or are away on a long-term guardian angel assignment.

We offer everything from karaoke to opera; mud wrestling to polo. Heavenly Productions is our theater company, which provides excellent entertainment. We have a resounding talent pool here, as you might expect. For instance, it is quite amazing to new arrivals to see William Shakespeare perform with Lawrence Olivier while Elvis accompanies them.

Whatever your wish, we have the museum you need. Libraries abound and sports stadiums are easily accessible by our Skyway Cab system, so there is never a problem getting to a stadium. Concerts of every type of music are held at the stadiums when no games are scheduled.

It is necessary to have tickets prior to an event because our marketing department likes to keep track of interest and participation at these events. There has never been a time when all who wished to attend a certain event or concert could not gain entry; the tickets are simply our way of pleasing the marketers without inconveniencing you. When you decide what you would like to do, simply enter your selection into a Request Box. Please allow up to five hours for your tickets to be delivered directly to your cloudlette. It pays to plan ahead!

Clothing

Clothing is optional, however, 82 percent of residents wear the heavenly issue T-shirt and slacks or shorts available on request through your Request Box. You have a choice of twenty colors, but the overwhelming favorite is white. Celestial shoes, similar to sneakers, but more cushiony and durable than those on Earth, are available in coordinating colors.

(*Note:* A small percentage of our clothing wearers, perhaps 3 percent, elect to wear our Flowing Robe, which is only available in white. Most of these persons also choose to go barefoot. The choice is, of course, entirely yours.)

The Phase System

While everyone is equal in Heaven, there is a "Phase System." This is not at all like a caste system. It refers to one's acclimation to, and progression in, Heaven. The following definitions should assist you in comprehending this system:

Newly Arrived (N.A.)—This is the initial phase. It is automatic and applies to all new arrivals. The length of time spent as an N.A. depends solely upon the individual. As an N.A., you are accorded all of the rights and privileges of Heaven, with the exception of G.A. (Guardian Angel) school and attendance at the Annual Angel Convention (a very, very large event).

Angel—This is a natural phase progression. It is, actually, the only direction an N.A. can take. Angel status is awarded once total Acceptance is achieved (as ascertained by a board of your peers) and you pass your handbook quiz. The quiz may be taken as many times as you see fit, there is no limit; however, you must pass it. The goal is to become a proficient Angel. As an Angel, you have all of the rights and privileges you had as an N.A. plus the option of either attending G.A. school or training to be a Reborn. You may also attend the Annual Angel Convention, a very prestigious affair. It is the angels who are responsible for the day-to-day smooth functioning of Heaven. As you can imagine, angels are very busy.

Guardian Angel (G.A.)—After becoming an Angel, you may elect to enter Guardian Angel school to participate in the training required to become a shepherd angel (more popularly known as a Guardian Angel). It should be noted that Guardian Angels are not always completely successful in their efforts. (Example: It has been found by the G.A. Review Committee (2006) that 42 percent of all traffic accidents on Earth are the direct result of one or more G.A.'s involvement, albeit with the best of intentions, because they did not know their right from their left. You most likely have seen evidence of this on every highway in the world. The reason has yet to be determined: is it inherent in those who choose to become G.A.s or is it something that happens during the training of a G.A.? Numerous studies are being conducted to correct this situation. In the interim, each G.A. is issued two soft, colored cotton wrist bands: red is for left [port] and green is for right [starboard]. We believe this program has been helpful to some degree.)

Reborn—Once Angel status is achieved, the option to become a Reborn always exists. This option requires extensive training.

Please note the following in summation:

Angels, therefore, have two choices, and only two: G.A. School or Reborning Training. Angels must do one or the other; they can remain mere angels for only five years, after which they must make their choice. Heaven will tolerate no slug-abouts.

If Reborning is chosen and the training begun, angels then are required to read the Heavenly Personals, a voluminous tome where impending births and family statistics are outlined. It is from these worldwide families that the angel chooses his Reborning family, fills in the appropriate forms, and submits him or herself to the Reborning Platform at the arranged time after the assignment is approved. There are a myriad of reasons one might choose particular circumstances in which to be reborn and you will learn these during your training. Suffice it to say, it truly does make sense. Perhaps to make it easier to comprehend, a person is not only expected, but also required, to experience "every living, Earthly experience available" before he/she can become a Winged Angel, the pen-ultimate and end-of-the-line phase.

Winged Angel—This is the final, ultimate designation. A Winged Angel is easily identified. These, and only these, are the ones with wings. (*Note:* Once in a while you might see a tiny winglet on an angel, but these are temporary, perhaps given as a special award for some super-nice deed above and beyond the call of duty.)

Once you are a Winged Angel, that is it. It means you have successfully experienced all Earthly circumstances, good and awful and/or earned your wing points as a Guardian Angel in superior standing. It is completely up to each individual just how long the road is to Winged Angelhood.

Fallen Angel—Yes, we must mention that there are those who, upon rebirth, so screw it up that they go elsewhere. This is why one must study the Heavenly Personals with a fine-tooth comb.

Age

This is one of the most difficult concepts to understand for our N.A.s. One's age is given such paramount importance on Earth in the form of birthday celebrations; driving age; drinking age; voting age; acting your age (whatever that means); Middle Age; Retirement Age, Golden Age, Second Childhood and so on. Because a part of a person's identity has previously been defined by his chronological age, many new arrivals (N.A.s) are disconcerted and always overjoyed to discover there is no such thing as age here in Heaven. Everyone is ageless!

Appearance/Condition

Please remember that it is your essence (spirit, soul, karma, whatever term you care to use) that resides in Heaven. This is uniquely yours and identifies you to others, others to you. This is the recognizable you, that which makes you different from all others. This essence is what you formerly recognized as *personality* or *personhood* in each individual. It never, ever ceases to exist, but continues to grow until you become a Winged Angel and your essence is complete. It is how you are recognized in Heaven by all who knew you and by those who are just coming to know you.

Therefore, it follows naturally that you are no longer subject to any physical pain, sickness, or discomfort of any sort. Whatever physical and/or mental ailments or pain you brought to the Main Gate is completely gone upon entry. (*Note:* There is no such thing as a practicing doctor, dentist, clinic, or hospital here. Most of the former doctors and dentists are too busy playing golf or fishing anyway.)

The Flag

Most new arrivals are enthralled and quite impressed with Heaven's flag, which encompasses every color of the rainbow and is mounted on a two-hundred-foot tall gold and jewel-encrusted flagpole at the center of the Main Reception Area. Similar flags on similar, but shorter, golden poles can be seen throughout Heaven. Each new arrival is presented a complimentary Flag O'Heaven on a small jeweled stand along with the words to "Flag O'Heaven" (sung to the tune of "Pomp and Circumstance").

Heavenly Songs

In addition to "Flag O'Heaven," most often sung at the daily new-arrival event in the Main Reception Area, there is no single anthem for Heaven. People sing all day long here. Every Earthly tune is, of course, remembered. However, there are many songs adapted to Earthly tunes, but whose words are Heaven-specific. The following are a few examples:

Example 1: "Praise to Our Heavenly Home"
Tune: "My Old Kentucky Home"
This song is the one performed most often prior to sporting and cultural events.

Example 2: "Welcome to Heaven"
Tune: "Shout! Shout!" (Isley Brothers version)
This lively tune is the one most often sent over our sound system in the Main Reception Area inside the Main Gate after "Flag O'Heaven" is sung at our daily New Arrivals Greeting Ceremonies.

Example 3: "Guardian Angels Together"
Tune: "Light My Fire" (The Doors's version)
This lively tune is sung both before and after any Guardian Angel meeting or event. It is always performed with a great deal of enthusiasm.

Example 4: "The Reborn Lullaby"
Tune: "Happy Trails" (Roy Rogers)
This song is the most popular one used to wish the reborner well as he/she waits on the Reborning Platform.

Example 5: "Love and Happiness"
Tune: "A Chorus Line"
General popular tune most often whistled

Example 6: "Thank Heaven"
Tune: "Bolero" (Ravel version)
Usually the first song new arrivals learn because of its oft-repeated, hence more easily learned, words and catchy rhythm

Example 7: "Bliss"
Tune: "Trumpet Voluntary in D" (Purcell version)
This is a happy, joyful song so appropriate for our happy, joyful crowd.

This small selection of tunes endemic to Heaven should suffice. There is a complete, and large, songbook available through your Request Box.

Money

Unnecessary, useless, obsolete. You don't need it. All of your needs are met at no cost to you. This is a priceless existence.

Acceptance

Acceptance is defined as "the quality or state of recognizing and agreeing, expressly and by conduct, to one's existence in Heaven." (Universal Dictionary, special heavenly volume)

There is, understandably, a transition period for every new arrival (N.A.). Every individual who comes to us is unique and, therefore, each person's adjustment time is unique.

Acceptance can take as little as a day, but we have had some cases where Acceptance has not occurred sooner than one year. Generally, Acceptance is accomplished between two and eight months after arrival.

For those who wish, there are Acceptance Centers with counselors on duty twenty-four hours a day. It is common for sudden-death N.A.s to experience the highest percentage of Acceptance difficulty.

Main Reception Area

This was the first place you saw when you entered the Main Gate. All new arrivals are "rung in" with great and exuberant fanfare by an attending angel, who rings a sixteen-foot high bell made of the purest crystal. It is customary to bring in new arrivals once each day. Only when the daily count is extremely high is a second group permitted to enter on the same day, such as during war times or as a result of natural disasters. This restriction makes sense, because there is a lot of paperwork and organization involved for the arrivals. Heaven likes to keep things as calm and smooth as possible. Arrivals at all times of the day would create havoc. Havoc is not a desired condition in Heaven.

Tours

Most new arrivals wish to explore Heaven, as do many of our other residents. We are continually expanding in all areas, especially our living areas. Available tours include guided walking tours; river and lake cruises; tram tramps; and airship adventures. If you prefer to arrange a self-guided walking tour, you can secure maps and other helpful items at any of our HH (Heavenly Highways) offices.

For overnight tours in outlying areas, we offer a wide range of C & Cs (cloudlette and coffees), campgrounds with all services; and motel and hotel accommodations. Reservations are not necessary as accommodations of all types are abundant.

Drifting

While Heaven requires participation and interaction among its residents, every one is afforded an extensive amount of free time. Drifting is a popular leisure activity. DriftWorld is similar to Earth's theme parks, such as Busch Gardens or Disneyland, and is easily accessible. There is always room at DriftWorld and no reservations are necessary.

At DriftWorld, you can relax on special soft clouds, lie back and let the cloud drift gently to the accompaniment of soft harp music in the distance. The clouds are programmable and automatically return you to your place of embarkment. Please be assured, you cannot float away!

All reports indicate that drifting is one of our residents' favorite pastimes. It is this activity that has gotten so much "press" on Earth.

Until recently, DriftWorld offered only daylight hours. However, as a result of strong requests from our Night People, we are proud to announce that DriftWorld is now open on a 24-hour basis for your drifting pleasure. We are open 364 days per year, closing only on Repair Day (in October) for cloud and harp maintenance.

Shopping

Rare is the resident who does not go shopping for something. Our New Arrivals are the most susceptible to the activity. Heavenly shops have EVERYTHING you could possibly want as well as items you never realized you were craving. In addition to our department stores, there are a variety of specialized boutiques for each individual taste.

Shopping centers are conveniently located to all resident cloudlettes. For those who don't wish to go to the shopping areas, Heaven offers a free delivery service, catalog shopping, online ordering and ten easy shop-at-home channels on your Earth Views Receiver (EVR). However you choose to shop, Heaven guarantees your satisfaction in all purchases. We take great pride in the fact that no one has ever found the need to exchange or return an item. There is never a price tag and supplies are unlimited on all items.

 The Halo

No one in Heaven has one; and, by unanimous popular vote, no one in Heaven wants one. A halo is a stylized symbol typically employed by artists on Earth in an effort to depict special spiritual attributes in their art. A halo in Heaven is a redundancy. *Note:* Many millennia ago, halos were issued on a trial basis; however, as a result of a special vote, the angels in Heaven were 100 percent against their continued use. Why? The answer is simple: Halos have an annoying tendency to get caught on too many things and, thereby, to inhibit freedom of movement. Additionally, halo maintenance is extremely time consuming, thus rendering them impractical and undesirable. We on the Heavenly Welcoming Committee are happy to announce that, for more than three million Earth years, there has been no further suggested legislation for the reinstitution of the halo in Heaven. (We have, alas, no control over their continued use by artists on Earth.)

The Divine Palace

This is the crown jewel and focal point in Heaven yet such a low profile is maintained, there is not much written about it. Our Great and Glorious One (aka many and various names) is in residence every moment of every day. Not a day goes by when our Great and Glorious One is not at work both in Heaven and on Earth. The Divine Palace has guided Heaven and Earth throughout recorded history (and before); it will continue to do so ad infinitum.

It should be noted: As busy as the Divine Palace is, time is always available to our residents. However, in this one case, appointments have become necessary. Please request such through your nearest Request Box. You may have to wait as long as two days for your appointment. Remember: patience is a virtue.

(*Note:* Every New Arrival [N.A.] is accorded a preliminary appointment during which all of his/her questions are answered.)

Welcome to Heaven!

We have done everything in our collective power to assure you an easy transition period and ecstatically beautiful time with us. However, if there is anything you desire or if you have any questions, do not hesitate to contact any one of us by telephone, through your Request Box, or in writing. We are here for your peace of mind and wealth of spirit. Again, a warm, Heavenly welcome!

Heavenly Welcoming Committee, 2007

LaVergne, TN USA
26 October 2009
161983LV00002B/25/A